KATHERINE GARBERA

CALLING ALL THE SHOTS

If you purchased this book without a cover you should be aware that this book is stolen property. It was reported as "unsold and destroyed" to the publisher, and neither the author nor the publisher has received any payment for this "stripped book."

Recycling programs for this product may not exist in your area.

ISBN-13: 978-0-373-73209-8

CALLING ALL THE SHOTS

Copyright © 2012 by Katherine Garbera

All rights reserved. Except for use in any review, the reproduction or utilization of this work in whole or in part in any form by any electronic, mechanical or other means, now known or hereafter invented, including xerography, photocopying and recording, or in any information storage or retrieval system, is forbidden without the written permission of the publisher, Harlequin Enterprises Limited, 225 Duncan Mill Road, Don Mills, Ontario M3B 3K9, Canada.

This is a work of fiction. Names, characters, places and incidents are either the product of the author's imagination or are used fictitiously, and any resemblance to actual persons, living or dead, business establishments, events or locales is entirely coincidental.

This edition published by arrangement with Harlequin Books S.A.

For questions and comments about the quality of this book, please contact us at CustomerService@Harlequin.com.

® and TM are trademarks of Harlequin Enterprises Limited or its corporate affiliates. Trademarks indicated with ® are registered in the United States Patent and Trademark Office, the Canadian Trade Marks Office and in other countries.

www.Harlequin.com

Printed in U.S.A.

Books by Katherine Garbera

Harlequin Desire

††*Reunited...With Child* #2079
The Rebel Tycoon Returns #2102
§§*Ready for Her Close-up* #2160
§§*A Case of Kiss and Tell* #2177
§§*Calling All the Shots* #2196

Silhouette Desire

‡‡*In Bed with Beauty* #1535
‡‡*Cinderella's Christmas Affair* #1546
‡‡*Let It Ride* #1558
Sin City Wedding #1567
‡‡*Mistress Minded* #1587
‡‡*Rock Me All Night* #1672
†*His Wedding-Night Wager* #1708
†*Her High-Stakes Affair* #1714
†*Their Million-Dollar Night* #1720
The Once-A-Mistress Wife #1749
***Make-Believe Mistress* #1798
***Six-Month Mistress* #1802
***High-Society Mistress* #1808
**The Greek Tycoon's Secret Heir* #1845
**The Wealthy Frenchman's Proposition* #1851
**The Spanish Aristocrat's Woman* #1858
Baby Business #1888
§*The Moretti Heir* #1927
§*The Moretti Seduction* #1935
§*The Moretti Arrangement* #1943
Taming the Texas Tycoon #1952
‡*Master of Fortune* #1999
‡*Scandalizing the CEO* #2007
‡*His Royal Prize* #2014
††*Taming the VIP Playboy* #2068
††*Seducing His Opposition* #2074

‡‡King of Hearts
†What Happens in Vegas…
**The Mistresses
*Sons of Privilege
§Moretti's Legacy
‡The Devonshire Heirs
††Miami Nights
§§Matchmakers, Inc.

Other titles by this author available in ebook format

KATHERINE GARBERA

is a *USA TODAY* bestselling author of more than forty books who has always believed in happy endings. She lives in England with her husband, children and their pampered pet, Godiva. Visit Katherine on the web at www.katherinegarbera.com, or catch up with her on Facebook and Twitter.

This book is dedicated to my family.
I know that I thank them a lot, but without them I don't think I'd want to tell stories with happy endings. So a big thank-you to Rob, Courtney, Lucas, Mom and Dad.

Acknowledgments

It feels wrong not to mention once again how wonderful my editor Charles Griemsman is and how much fun I have chatting with him about stories! Thank you for your guidance and insight.

One

Most days Willow Stead loved her job. She felt very lucky to be pretty much her own boss. But not today.

The problem had actually started months ago, when the network bigwigs had pulled some strings and gotten the second most popular television host in America to work on her show. Great, right?

Not if that man was Jack Crown.

Sure, he was good-looking and charming. But beneath that toothy grin and effervescent personality beat the heart of a rogue. While his type of bad boy could be redeemed on TV or on the pages of a romance novel, in real life he couldn't. Which was something Willow knew firsthand, having had her heart broken by this very man at the tender age of sixteen.

"Drinks, Willow, that's all I'm suggesting," Jack was saying with that sexy smile of his.

There was no doubting why he'd been named one

of *People's* Sexiest Men Alive for the past four years. But she was resistant to his appeal. *Yeah, right.* If only the callousness she remembered—he'd stood her up on prom night, for Pete's sake—was enough to keep her from falling for him.

She'd done her best to keep her distance from him over the past six months as they'd worked together on *Sexy & Single,* the New York–based reality TV matchmaking show she was producing. But she couldn't deny she wanted to accept his invitation for drinks.

"Um…you haven't said no yet, so I guess you need me to talk you into it," he said, his voice dropping to an intimate whisper. "Is that what you want?"

"What I want is for you to stop acting like I'm one of your rotating harem," she said, trying for disdain. "I'm not like all the other women that fall at your feet."

"Ah, you've wounded me," he said, clutching at where his heart should be.

"Doubtful," she said. "But since we do need to discuss the show, I'll accept."

"Geez, Willow, don't sound so eager," he said. "There was a time when you used to enjoy being with me."

She wrinkled her nose at him. She didn't like being reminded of her past infatuation. God, could she have been more obvious back then? If she could write a letter to her sixteen-year-old self, she'd start it with STOP MOONING OVER JACK CROWN! and be done with it.

"I'm not that girl anymore," she said.

"I don't believe that," he said. "I still see shades of her in how you act with everyone but me. Why is that? Clearly I've done something to rub you the wrong way."

"Just because I'm not buying your public image doesn't mean anything," she said. "Gail has told me enough about PR for me to know that you can't be America's Sweetheart in real life."

Gail Little was one of Willow's best friends and had been the reason Willow had pitched the idea of this show to her bosses at the network. Gail's personal matchmaking experience had been captured on the first episodes of *Sexy & Single*—her dates with New Zealand billionaire playboy Russell Holloway had really brought in the viewers. The quiet, sophisticated Gail taming the wild Russell had been ratings gold.

"Forget image. You know me," he said. "What do you believe?"

He didn't want to know, and there was no way she was opening that can of worms. "I don't know you. Not really. You spend more time flying cross-country to host your other shows than here on the set with me. But that doesn't matter. So what about those drinks?"

He rolled his eyes. "I'll buy you dinner *and* drinks if you stop evading the question and tell me what's going on. We've been working together for six months and I keep getting the cold shoulder from you. I must be remembering our high school years differently because I thought we'd been friends."

"You must be," she said. "Can we eat out without your legions of fans finding us?"

"No," he said. "But I have an apartment that's a short walk from here. What do you say? Want to come back to my place?"

She started to shake her head but then stopped. She did want to have dinner with him. A part of her was hoping he'd be interested in her so she could date and dump him the way he'd dumped her the night of prom. She knew it was petty and she didn't like that about herself but she'd never been a turn-the-other-cheek person. *Never.*

She'd waited for the perfect moment to get her revenge. And it looked like it had arrived a mere fourteen years later… Who said that patience wasn't rewarded?

"Okay, I'll do it," Willow said. Maybe she could include a little anecdote about how Jack got his comeuppance in that letter to her sixteen-year-old self.

"Good. How long until you're done here?" he asked.

"About twenty minutes. I have to talk to the camera crew. They had a problem on the shoot last night. Why don't you leave me the address and I'll meet you there," she said.

"You're not going to back out, are you?"

"That's not my plan. I said I'd be there."

"Good. I thought I remembered you as a girl of your word," he said. There was a natural confidence about him that was so attractive—too bad that she hated it. She wanted to see some cracks in the facade of America's Sweetheart. She wanted to see that life threw him curveballs once in a while.

"Jack?"

"Hmm?"

"Women don't like to be referred to as girls," she said.

"My bad," he said with a wink.

"You're about to have an epic fail if you do it again."

He laughed as he turned to walk away. She couldn't help staring at his fine backside until he disappeared through the door.

"Looks like hell might be in danger of freezing over," Nichole Reynolds said as she approached Willow.

"Shut up," Willow said to her other best friend. Nichole was the pop culture reporter for *America Today,* the national newspaper, and wrote a behind-the-scenes blog for the show. And she was one of the few people who knew the truth about Jack.

"Just saying. And you should be nicer to me, I'm about to be a mommy," Nichole said, patting her baby bump.

She had recently married Conner MacAfee, the owner of the matchmaking service featured on the show, and was expecting her first child. Nichole was truly happy with Conner, and Willow was glad for her friend.

"I have to be nice because you're pregnant?" Willow asked. The truth was there were two people in the world that Willow really cared about, and Nichole was one of them.

"It wouldn't hurt. So did I hear correctly—you're having dinner with Jack Crown? What happened to wanting revenge on him?" Nichole asked.

"I still do," Willow admitted. "It's just dinner. Even I'm not so irresistible to make a man fall for me that quickly."

Oh, God, where had that come from? She wasn't that girl anymore. The one who'd been so happy that a popular boy had smiled at her.

"Oh, Willow, don't sell yourself short," Nichole said with a cheeky grin. "He is definitely interested in you."

"For now. It's just because I've been ignoring him. I bet if I let him woo me tonight, he'd lose interest," Willow said.

"I'll take that bet," Nichole said.

"What?"

"I bet he won't lose interest in you," Nichole said. "What do you want to wager?"

"Nothing. I'm not really betting on Jack," Willow said.

"Why not? You said he was shallow. What have you got to lose?" Nichole asked.

Her pride. What if she fell for him a second time and had to watch him walk away again? She didn't want to be the loser in a relationship with him—twice. "I was being flip."

"No, you weren't. Come on, I'll bet you a spa day at Elizabeth Arden Red Door," Nichole said.

"No fair, you know I love that place," Willow said. "Why are you insisting on this?"

Nichole wrapped her arm around Willow's shoulder. "You can't trust any man because of that one incident with Jack so long ago. I want to see you healed from that so you can find a guy and settle down like Gail and I did. We're happy and we want you to be, too."

She hugged her friend back. A part of her wanted that, too. "I just want him to feel the pain I felt."

"I don't care what the outcome is as long as you can move on," Nichole said.

"Okay, I'll take the bet. But you're going to lose and I'm going to gloat," Willow said.

"Fine by me, but if he stays interested in you, then I win, and I'm going to save my spa day until after the baby comes."

"Fair enough," Willow said. "But they'll be ice skating in hell before I fall for Jack Crown."

"You keep telling yourself that," Nichole said. "It will make my victory that much sweeter."

November in New York had a certain excitement to it. Not that the City ever lacked energy but there was something about this time of year when everyone and everything seemed to be gearing up for Christmas.

For Jack, it was the beginning of one of his busiest times of the year. He had three holiday specials that needed to be filmed—they were all live tapings. Plus a year-end recap show of *Extreme Careers,* his series that was otherwise already in the can. His agent was on him about his next big gig and Jack knew he was moving into another phase of his career. Finally he didn't have to drum up work—producers and networks were coming to him.

Since he was so busy it didn't surprise him that this was when Willow finally accepted a date with him. It was just like her to make his life a little crazier. But then maybe that was why he'd been asking her out.

Jack looked around his apartment, making sure every detail was perfect. It wasn't so much that he was nervous—hey, he was Jack Crown and every woman wanted to be with him—but this was Willow. He couldn't say for sure when he'd become so obsessed with her.

He suspected it was because unlike every other girl he met, she just…treated him like he was part of her crew. No special smiles, no attempts to get him alone. He knew that shouldn't bother him. But it did.

He had faint memories of her from high school when she'd tutored him in language arts so he wouldn't fail the state test and could continue to play football. But that was all. Just flashes of a younger Willow interspersed with his football-playing days.

Back then football was his life. Considering he'd grown up in Texas on the poorer side of town, there was only one real ticket out of poverty for him—sports. He'd gone on to be a Heisman Trophy–winning wide receiver and then a first-round draft pick for the New York Giants. Unfortunately, his first time-out he'd been brought down by a career-ending tackle. He'd learned after his injury that he was going to have to find something else to do and quick. Luckily he'd always had an affinity for being on camera and had been able to segue into a broadcasting gig.

The buzzer rang and he hurried over to answer it. His converted loft building had a state-of-the-art security system. When he hit a button, a small black-and-white screen showed Willow standing at the outside door.

He buzzed her in and then glanced around the apartment to make sure everything was in order. He didn't have to be a rocket scientist to know that Willow wasn't going to give him another chance at getting this right. This working date had to be perfect.

There was a knock on the door and he smiled to himself as he crossed to open it. He planned on knocking her socks off and ensuring that when she left his apartment—preferably in the morning—she'd be dying to see him again.

Willow had an earthy sensuality about her that made him more aware of her sexually each time they met. At first, he'd just wanted to rekindle their old friendship, but as she'd continued to ignore him, she'd awakened something primal inside of him. He suspected an affair with Willow would affect their working relationship, but at this point he knew his ego would settle for nothing less than having her. He needed to prove to both of them that she'd made a mistake by ignoring him.

He opened the door and Willow scowled up at him. She looked tired and thin, something he hadn't noticed when they were on the set or even in the editing booth. She always moved with so much energy, but tonight she seemed worn out.

Not exactly the right mood he needed her in. But he'd grown up with a single mom and had learned early on how to cheer her up with a lot of attention. So he shifted gears in his head.

He pulled her close for a hug, rubbing her back. But she wedged her arms between them. "What are you doing?"

"You looked like you needed a hug," he said, stepping back and leading her into his apartment. It wasn't overly luxurious like the apartment they'd photographed him at for *Architectural Digest* a few months back. He couldn't live like that. He supposed it was the small-town Texas boy in him but that kind of opulence made him feel out of place.

His loft was an open floor plan with a kitchen at one end and a huge entertainment area on the other. That was one thing he didn't mind splurging on. There were large comfortable couches as well as a nicely appointed dining area.

"I could use a drink," Willow said.

"Wine, beer or something stronger?" he asked. He had a fully stocked bar, even though he wasn't much of a drinker. He didn't like feeling out of control. He'd learned that after a brief stint of stupidity when he'd been recovering from his knee injury and had had no job prospects.

"What kind of wine do you have?" she asked.

"Just about every kind. I endorse a vineyard and they send me a case of everything they make," he said with a wry grin.

"That's right. You're everyone's favorite ad man. I like dry white wine," she said.

"Coming right up. Dinner will be ready in about ten minutes. Do you want to go out on the balcony?" he asked.

"It's cold outside," she said.

"I have those patio heaters. You'll be comfortable," he said.

She nodded and turned away from him. He watched her walk slowly across his apartment before he started toward the kitchen. She was on edge and didn't seem to be in the mood to enjoy this evening with him. If he was a different kind of man he'd give up but he was used to overcoming odds and coming out the winner. After all everyone said after his career-ending football injury that he was going to have to go back to Frisco, Texas. But he hadn't.

He poured them both a glass of wine and headed out to the balcony. It was quiet, thanks to the glass walls that surrounded the patio area, and warm, thanks to his heaters.

"Thanks," she said. "Sorry I was so snippy earlier."

"No problem," he said. He lifted his glass to hers. "To new beginnings."

"New beginnings," she said. "For tonight or since we met?"

Something about what she said made him realize that the past might hold the key to whatever the problem was between them. "For everything. I know I've changed since I left Frisco and I'm sure you have, too."

"Not as much as you'd think," she said, taking a sip of her wine. "I still love football and feel guilty if I don't go to church on Sunday. Though the Baptist church I attend here is nothing like Prestonwood back home."

He chuckled. No state did religion like Texas. "I know what you mean. My mom is praying for my soul since I'm usually working and don't get to church as often as I should."

"Sinner. You're such a bad boy," she said, but there was a grin on her face when she said it.

"Haven't I always been?"

"Yes, you have. Tell me about the new Jack Crown. What haven't I seen?" she asked.

He started to talk about himself but stopped. He wasn't sure why but he knew that going on and on about his TV shows and his lifestyle wasn't the right tack with Willow. "I'm not interested in that. Tell me about you. I remember in high school you wanted to be a writer."

He saw the momentary surprise in her eyes before she masked it. She turned away from him, took another sip of her wine and then cleared her throat. "That's right, I did, but once I got to school I realized that I'm more into telling people what to do."

He grinned as he suspected she wanted him to. But he'd been a star athlete and had lost the ability to play his game so he knew that dreams—especially those that were held since childhood—were hard to let go of. "I'm glad it was easy for you to transition. It wasn't for me."

"From football?" she asked. "I saw the game where you were injured and despite everything I felt bad about what happened."

"What do you mean despite everything?" he asked.

"Just that I wasn't a Giants fan," she said.

Again he sensed there was more she wasn't saying but this was a first date so that made sense. He'd find out what she was hiding from him as time went on.

The timer on his iPod beeped and he stood up. "Dinner's ready."

"I think I'll go wash up," she said. "Can you direct me to the restroom?"

"To the left of the TV wall," he said. "I'll give you a tour after dinner."

She arched one eyebrow at him. "What else would you show me except your bedroom…the entire apartment is visible?"

"I'll show you my bedroom," he said. "But I'll wait until you ask to see it."

"Don't hold your breath," she said.

"Over dinner I want you to explain why you're so prickly," he said.

"Just because I'm not swooning at the thought of seeing your bedroom?" she asked.

"Sort of. But you also seem to be almost angry at me and I don't know why," he said.

"Oh, I…"

"Not now. Go wash up and while we're eating you can tell me. I'm very good at fixing things," he said.

She shook her head. "Not this."

He watched her walk away again and this time he was just as puzzled by her as the first time. He wanted her, which was why he'd been trying so hard to convince her to go out with him. But now that she was here and he realized how much of herself she kept hidden from the world…well, it just intrigued him more.

He wanted to get to know the whole Willow not just seduce her into his bed. But both objectives were looking harder than he'd thought they'd be.

There was definitely something from their mutual past that he'd done to upset her. But for the life of him he couldn't put his finger on what it was. He rarely thought of those old days now.

He got the dinner his housekeeper had prepared out of the oven and set the table for two. Willow still hadn't emerged from the bathroom and he wondered why.

He was about to go knock on the door when she was back with a fake bright smile on her face. "Dinner smells good. I had no idea you could cook."

"I can't," he said.

"Another illusion shattered," she said.

"I never said I could cook," he said.

"I know. It's just that you seem like you can do everything," she said. "All the shows and the easy charm. Life just looks really good for you."

"It is, but that doesn't mean it's easy. I have struggles like everyone else."

He held her chair out and she sat down at the table. "Jack Crown isn't like everyone else."

"I was hoping you'd see that. I'm not like any other man you know," he said. "But I think you meant that in a negative way. So tell me—what did I do to make you so angry?"

She swallowed hard and looked up at him with those big, dark brown eyes of hers. "Nothing. I've just been burned in the past by men who seemed too good to be true."

"Get to know me so you can see that I'm exactly what you think I am."

"That might not work in your favor," she said. "I don't have a positive impression of you."

"I can work with it," he said. He always had the feeling that she was judging him, and if there was one thing he knew about Willow it was that she didn't pull her punches or her words. "How would you describe me?"

"Too charming for your own good," she said.

"I can work with charming," he said.

Two

"Not charming. *Too* charming," she reminded him.

Willow hadn't meant to reveal how she felt about Jack but she realized that she couldn't help herself. Yes, she wanted some kind of revenge on him but she also wanted him to know how she felt. She wanted him to have a clue about her distrust of him. She almost would have said she disliked him but she knew that was a lie.

"Too charming…that can mean a myriad of things," he said. "Do you find me irresistible?"

"Never," she said. "You do have moments when I think I could like you but then your ego comes shining through."

"It's hard to be humble when I've got so much going for me," he said.

It took a minute for her to get that he was teasing her. She really didn't want to like him. It was okay to see flashes of it but she didn't want to see that there was a real man behind the toothy grin and perfectly styled hair.

"Yeah, you got it all," she said. "I know you're being silly but to someone on the outside it looks like you do live a charmed life. Why would you be interested in me?" she asked. No sense in beating around the bush. It was the one thing that seemed illogical to her. He could have any woman he wanted so why her? Why now?

"Maybe because you're a challenge," he said.

It was the answer she was expecting but disappointing all the same. "So it's just a game to you then?"

"Not a game. Life is too short to not go after what you want. I like you. You can be funny on the set and I see the way you really connect with the couples and with your friends and crew. I want to be a part of that."

She didn't know what he meant. Sure she made the time to listen to people but only because she'd learned that if she didn't then the results they got when filming weren't that great. "That's just the way I work."

"It's more than that. I saw you holding Bella McCaw when Fiona needed someone to take care of her. And there was a look on your face…."

Fiona was a fashion designer and single mom who'd come on the show with her darling daughter, Bella Ann. She'd been matched to Alex Cannon, a games developer. They were an interesting couple who were now happily engaged.

"What look?" she asked. She always liked to believe she had a poker face that didn't reveal what she was thinking. Wasn't that true?

He shrugged. "It just got me to thinking that I wanted to get to know you better."

"Are you looking to settle down with me?" she asked. If he said yes, it would really give her the ammunition she needed to bring him to his knees. But on the other hand…he wasn't the boy she knew in high school. Maybe he didn't deserve her vengeance.

"No," he said. "Just want to get to know you better. For a few moments I want to be like every other man in America who has an attractive coworker and invites her out for dinner."

"You're never going to be like every other man in America. You know that, right?" How could he look at his life and think he could be like everyone else? He'd won a Heisman Trophy. They only gave out one a year, so that put him in an elite sportsman category. He'd been named Associated Press Athlete of the Year and played professional football before going on to be the host of some of the most popular shows on TV. He was never going to be an average Joe.

"Yes, I do, but with you I feel like I am. All the trappings of the celebrity lifestyle aren't important to you," he said.

"That's true. I've seen the other side of celebrity," she said.

"Me, too. We are uniquely suited for each other," he said, waggling his eyebrows and smiling over at her.

"I don't know." She did know. If she played this right she could get him thinking that maybe he could have something with her. Then she'd walk away.

"Come on, how many people do you meet in this business from Frisco, Texas?" he said with that half smile of his that reminded her a little too much of the boy who'd first stolen her heart.

She put down her fork and took a sip of her wine. Revenge, she thought. She had to stay focused on what she really wanted or she was going to lose her way.

He reached over and touched her hand. A little zing

shot up her arm. His touch unnerved her as much now as it had when he'd hugged her earlier. He ran his finger over her knuckles and then turned her hand over in his and traced the lines on her palm.

"I'm only asking for a chance here," he said.

A chance. To do what? He'd said he wanted a regular relationship but had never had a chance to have that because of his celebrity.

And she wanted what Nichole had suggested. A chance to find some happiness for herself down the line. So she had to do something with Jack. Had to find a way to make peace with her past so she could trust again. And she knew now that unless he was hiding cloven hooves and the devil's tail she wasn't going to be able to be as coldly calculating as she'd thought she could be. She'd thought that focusing on getting back at him would be enough to protect her but maybe it wasn't.

"A chance, eh? Just dating?" she asked. She didn't want to admit it—even to herself—but the thought of walking away from him was beginning to fade.

"Yes, dating. It's not going to be easy since I have to fly back and forth between the coasts all the time but I do want a chance to get to know you better. A chance to prove that there is more to me than Prince Charming."

"I've never called you Prince Charming," she said.

"Everyone knows I am," he said with that stupid arrogant grin of his. "Let's face it, you even said I was charming."

Suddenly she thought it might not be too hard to hurt him if he was going to act like this. Was this the real Jack Crown? She had no idea, and she never would unless she took a chance on him.

"Fine, we can date," she said. But as she looked into those very blue eyes of his, she couldn't help a niggling sensation that this was a bad idea. She was susceptible to Jack. She always had been. And she knew how easy it was to fall for him.

Wanting revenge was one thing, but messing up her life at work—the one place where she was truly at home and happy—didn't seem smart. If she was going to fool around with Jack and walk away, she had to be careful how she timed it and that she never let it interfere with work.

"Golly gee, Willow, don't sound so excited about it," he said.

She nodded over at him. "I'm sorry. I'd be happy to go on dates with you when the time allows."

"That's all I ask," he said, tracing a random pattern on her palm before closing his fingers over it.

She knew he wanted something more from her and only if she kept her wits about her would she be able to protect herself from being hurt once again by Jack Crown.

Jack felt like he was playing a part for Willow. If he had a hope in hell of making this real, he had to stop. The problem was he no longer knew who he was. It had been his problem for a while now and while it was easy to admit to himself that he was coasting through life, it was hard to figure out how to change.

Willow was the key, he thought. Watching her on the set of *Sexy & Single* had been the catalyst. He did want something more from her. He wanted to feel like he was alive again. He was tired from working all the time and taking silly risks on *Extreme Careers* to make himself remember he was alive.

They had finished dinner and he'd cleared the table with Willow's help. He liked having her in the kitchen because it strongly reminded him of happy days from his youth. Not one of the women he'd dated in the past year had come into his kitchen when he'd had them over for dinner.

Another thing that had set Willow apart was that she hadn't pulled out her smartphone one time during their meal. Despite her initial reluctance to join him for dinner, she hadn't been distracted by the outside world once she did.

He put the last of the dishes on the counter and turned, leaning back against it to watch her. She glanced over at him and he could see he'd startled her.

"Why are you looking at me like that?" she asked.

He felt like he had to constantly be on his guard around her. She didn't just relax and let herself enjoy the night. She was waiting for something to happen. Something he was supposed to do, he suspected, but he had no idea what it was.

"I'm trying to figure out why you were so jumpy when I hugged you," he said.

She shrugged. "I…I just was. No need to dig deeper."

It was almost too easy to find out what made her tick. She gave away things he knew she didn't mean to with her defensive attitude. She was cool and casual when he was talking about things like work but anything the slightest bit personal and she got her back up.

"There is always a reason to dig deeper with you. You are hiding so much of the real Willow beneath a facade of calmness. You never show more than a hint of what's going on below the surface."

"That's because in our business only divas can get away with throwing a temper tantrum," she said, then arched her eyebrow at him. "Isn't that right?"

"Are you trying to say I'm a diva?"

"Not trying—I did. I wasn't the only one who heard the dressing-down you gave Kat last week when you didn't have an exotic fruit basket in your dressing room."

He almost flushed at the way she said it. "I was jet-lagged and I apologized later."

"I know. Kat's used to dealing with those types of situations so it didn't even faze her."

"Some days it's harder than others," he said. He wasn't proud of the way he'd behaved. It was difficult sometimes—when everyone wanted a piece of you—to remember he wasn't entitled to any of the fame he'd gotten. He tried to remind himself that his mom would have tanned his hide if she'd been alive to witness his ogreish behavior.

"What is? Being America's second most popular TV host?" she asked.

"You're being flip, but my management people and network bosses look at my Q rating every day. There is a lot of pressure to stay on top," he said. "Plus every time I step outside someone wants an autograph or to talk about my latest exploits…and I'm not complaining. I know without those people I'd be just another washed-up ball player. Still, as I said, some days it's harder than others."

She tipped her head to the side and studied him. "I know. That's why so many people in our business are so messed up. I bet you never thought you'd have these types of problems."

"Definitely not. I figured I'd play football until I was thirty and then retire with my trophy wife to a large ranch in Texas Hill Country, teaching my boys how to play," he said with a sardonic laugh. "This definitely wasn't part of my plans."

"Trophy wife? Why are you trying to date me then?"

she asked, crossing her arms under her breasts and giving him the same hard look she gave the cameramen when they didn't get a shot she wanted.

"I said that was my original idea of what my life would be. Things changed—I'm over thirty now," he said. Willow sort of did fit his idea of a trophy wife, though—she was sexy as hell, successful in her own right and she knew how to make things happen.

"Yes, you are, old man."

He liked it when she teased him. It was as if she forgot who he was outside of this apartment and she let herself relax.

"I'm not that ancient."

"Nope, but you'll always be older than me," she said with a smile. Her phone twittered in her pocket and she gave him a wry smile. "I've got to check that. It keeps going off, which makes me think it might be urgent."

"Go ahead," he said. "Would you like coffee or maybe an after dinner drink?"

"Coffee would be great," she said.

"You can go into the living room," he said. "I'll bring it in."

She nodded distractedly as she pulled her phone from her pocket and read the message she'd received. He noticed that she chewed on her lower lip and her brow furrowed as she read.

He watched as she settled herself on the overstuffed leather sofa he'd ordered from Italy last year before turning to make them both a cup of coffee. He carried the cups over and placed them on the coffee table, then sat down next to her on the couch. She was still tapping out a message on her phone.

The scent of her perfume was light and floral and reminded him of spring. He stretched his arm along the back of the couch and felt the cool fall of her straight hair against his hand. He wanted to reach out and touch it, to bury his fingers in her hair, but he didn't want to distract her. He liked being able to sit here and just watch her.

She sighed and then put her phone on the table. "Deidre is getting cold feet. She doesn't think that Peter is right for her and has asked for another match," Willow said.

"Can she do that?" he asked.

"I guess so. I've sent Mona a message to see what she can do," Willow said.

Mona was the matchmaker at Matchmakers, Inc. who was providing all the couples at the show. Jack was surprised that this couple was having such a hard time since Mona's instincts had been right for the other three couples that had gone before them.

Deidre Adamson was a very popular advice columnist and television talk show host who rose to fame by turning her brutal honesty on the people who came on her show. Jack liked that kind of straight shooting. She'd been matched with the famous Peter Mullen. He was wild and a bit outrageous.

"Peter must have done something that shook her," Jack said. "I've been chatting with him a bit on the set. Do you want me to see if I can step in and fix this?"

Willow just stared at him for a minute. This was her headache and she was used to fixing problems on her own. "How could you help?"

"I actually know Deidre," he said. "And I've had a couple of chats with Peter. My guess is that Peter said or did something that scared her."

"Like what?" Willow asked. She was a little embarrassed to admit that she didn't think that Jack was sensitive enough to notice anyone else, much less be aware that they had nuances.

"Well, Deidre talks tough on her show but in real life she's very sensitive. I'm betting Peter thinks she's tougher than she is and probably pushed her too fast."

"You think?" Willow asked. "Deidre seems very much in control and bossy to me. I was guessing she told Peter to do something and he didn't do it."

"Might be. They both like to be in charge," Jack said. "If she gets a new man, would we have to start all over again with them?"

"Yes. It would mean three weeks of wasted filming," Willow said. "Do you know Deidre well enough to call her up and chat with her?"

"Yes, I do."

"How do you know her? She doesn't move in the Hollywood circles you do," Willow said.

"She was my therapist after my accident. She was the one who helped steer me toward broadcasting."

Willow hadn't thought about how he'd transitioned to his current career. She'd just thought...well, that he was the golden boy so things worked out for him. She'd been a little jealous of how easy his life looked from her point of view but she was getting glimpses of him that made her realize Jack's life wasn't as effortless as it seemed.

"I'd love it if you would call and talk to her. Can you do it now? I'll text Mona and tell her to wait before she talks to Deidre."

"Yes, I can do it, but only if you promise you'll do me a favor in return," he said.

"Okay," she said.

"Don't you want to know what I want?"

"Nope. I need her to stay matched to Peter so I don't have to throw out three weeks worth of work."

Jack lifted one eyebrow at her. "Whatever I ask for you'll do?"

She would probably regret this. "Yes, a favor of your choosing."

"Good. Drink your coffee while I save the day," he said before going upstairs.

She stood up and walked around his apartment. She was surprised that his walls weren't lined with photos of himself and celebrities. He gave the impression that he'd have lots of those but there weren't any on display. Instead there was a painting by the celebrated Texan Charles Beckendorf. The craggy valleys of the Texas canyons provided a backdrop for a longhorn steer that stared out at the viewer.

She had one of his paintings hanging in her brownstone in Brooklyn. As soon as she'd started making real money she had decided to invest in art and had begun by supporting artists from her home state. She had also endowed a scholarship for girls from her high school.

She moved past the painting, feeling a little homesick for Texas after viewing it. Next was a picture she recognized from their high school yearbook. It was their state champion football team. She didn't have to search to find Jack in the photo since she knew exactly where he was—in the second row, center. His smile was wider than the Texas sky. Coach Masters stood in the middle of the group and all of the starters crowded around him.

"I've never been as happy as I was in that moment," Jack said, coming up behind her. He reached around her to run his finger over the trophy in the picture. "I thought that my life was set."

She glanced over at him. That photo had been earth-shattering for her as well. Seeing it had made her think, *This is it; I'm going to figure out how to hurt him like he hurt me.* But hearing Jack talk about it with a tinge of wistfulness in his voice, she realized that even back then his life hadn't been as perfect as she'd thought.

"What did Deidre say?" she asked. For Willow when life got too uncomfortable she turned to work. And thank God that she and Jack had a job in common.

He rubbed the back of his neck and then smiled at her. "She said she'd give him another chance. I think one of us, maybe you, should pull Peter aside and tell him to slow down just a little bit. He's going too fast for her."

"But that's how I get good TV," Willow said.

"I know, but if he doesn't he'll scare her off, and you don't want that, do you?"

"No, I don't," she said. "It'd be so much easier if we could script things for them. But I know that the viewers wouldn't enjoy it as much."

"You're right. Just think—you couldn't have scripted that moment when Alex Cannon first held little Bella Ann. That was pure heartwarming television. You could see him melt," Jack said.

"Yes, you could. And let's face it, if Gail and Russell, Alex and Fiona, and Rikki and Paul could make it work, so can Deidre and Peter. He must have something that she wants."

"He must," Jack said.

Willow glanced at her watch. It was almost nine. She should be going soon. But first she texted Mona to say that the problem had been solved and that there was no need for her to find another match for Deidre right now.

"I guess I should be heading home. We're shooting early tomorrow," she said.

"Before you go…" he said.

Damn, she should have known she wasn't going to get out the door without doing this.

"Yes?"

"You owe me a favor, remember?"

Of course she remembered. She had been so desperate to keep Deidre on the show that she'd acted rashly. Or had she? A part of her realized that she wanted to owe Jack something so that she'd have an excuse to keep on seeing him.

"So what exactly do you want from me?"

"A kiss."

Three

A kiss.

Really, she shouldn't be that surprised, and since he asked for it as a favor, she could just enjoy it guilt free. She'd be lying if she didn't admit that she had once spent an inordinate amount of time thinking about kissing him.

"Okay," she said, trying hard to sound blasé. But instead her voice did a squeaky thing and she felt as lame as she had in high school when he'd asked her to go to the Dairy Queen for a cone.

He laughed, but it wasn't unkind, and for the first time since she'd entered his apartment she felt like she was seeing a glimpse of the real man. Because in that laugh was a hint of her own nervousness. And that made him human. She got what he'd been trying to explain earlier—that despite the success and fame he'd found, at heart he was still just a regular guy.

"Are you sure? I don't want a repeat of when I tried to hug you," he said.

She nodded, not trusting her own voice. She wanted to kiss him. She'd never gotten a kiss back in high school and though she'd moved past living as that girl she still had an imaginary bucket list that included kissing Jack Crown.

He leaned down toward her and she tipped her head back, not realizing until they were this close how much taller he was than her. She closed her eyes as his hands settled on her shoulders and he drew her in toward him. Though their bodies didn't touch, she could feel his body heat.

She felt the warmth of his breath over her mouth first. It had the pleasant scent of the coffee he'd drunk after dinner. The brush of his lips over hers was exhilarating; she felt tingles from her lips down her neck and to the very core of her body.

It was a gentle start but not tentative at all. She sensed he was taking care not to scare her off.

His mouth opened slowly on hers and she held her breath, trying to analyze this moment so she could pull it out and examine it later, but thought was impossible as a wave of sensation rolled over her. He tasted perfect, and unlike some of the men she'd kissed in the past, there was no awkward desire to pull back from him.

He feathered his tongue lightly into her mouth as he massaged her shoulders and pulled her closer to him. Then his tongue went deeper into her mouth, until shivers of desire coursed through her body.

She felt like she was falling into a world where there was just Jack. She reached out for something to steady herself. Her hands brushed over his chest. It was strongly muscled and radiated warmth. Even through the fabric of his shirt she could feel it. His hands moved down her back to her waist and drew her in until they were pressed together.

She didn't want them to fit together the way they did. As if they were meant to hold each other this way. His kiss continued to inflame her senses. She loved the way his fingers felt at the back of her neck as they tangled in her hair.

He lifted his head and sighed. She opened her eyes to look up at him and was surprised by the look on his face. There was desire, of course, but something else. He framed her face with his hands and whispered her name before he kissed her again.

This embrace lacked the restraint of the first time. She couldn't think as passion swept over her. She went up on tiptoe so she could take more of his kiss. She wanted something more from him.

He caressed her neck and shoulders and then slid his hands down her back to cup her butt, pulling her tightly against him. She gasped at the feel of his erection pressing into her stomach and moisture pooled in her center. She had known she wanted him but this was different. This was white-hot desire and she was desperate to touch more of him.

To have more of him…more of Jack. She slid her hands under his shirt and up his back. His hands tightened on her as his tongue plunged deeper into her mouth. He shifted until he leaned back against the wall and she was supported fully by his weight.

He lifted his head, and she felt cold without his mouth pressed against hers.

"One kiss…I thought it would be enough, but I want more," he said.

She did, too, but this was Jack. And now that his

mouth wasn't on hers…she pushed away from him and he let her go, his hands trailing over her hips until they fell to his sides.

"That got out of hand," she said.

"I don't think so, but I guess you're not ready for anything more," he said.

She sensed the frustration behind his words and she felt it, too, but she wasn't going to rush things with Jack. She still didn't know how she felt about him, and instead of making matters clearer, this night had only served to muddle them.

"I'm sorry, but I can't rush into this. I thought you were a shallow me, me, me, guy when I came here tonight," she admitted.

"And now?"

"I'm not sure," she said. She wasn't sure about anything anymore. Revenge was something that she'd craved and giving it up just wasn't an option, but now she understood the saying about it being a dish best served cold. Because this heat between them melted her resolve.

"That's why I need some time to think about this," she said.

He nodded. "Fair enough. You'll have plenty of time to mull things over because I leave for L.A. after we finish shooting in the morning. I won't be back in New York for a week."

She felt a sense of loss at the thought of him leaving and she knew that she had to get her head straight. It was a good thing he was going away because right now she'd have to say she was still stupid where he was concerned. But she'd miss him. And she hadn't expected to.

"Will you have dinner with me again next Saturday?"

he asked. "Not here, but on a proper date where I pick you up and take you out."

"Yes," she said and her voice did that squeaky thing again. She shook her head. "Hopefully I'll be able to speak when you see me next week."

"I like you just the way you are, Willow."

She wished she could believe that was true, but he didn't know her. He hadn't back in high school and he didn't now. On the set she treated him the way she did all talent—with a certain indulgence coupled with disdain. But he was talking about liking her. How could he? She wasn't even sure she liked herself.

"Ah, you're just saying that…aren't you?" There was a hint of something fragile in her voice.

Jack felt as if Willow was still running away from him, and he knew no matter what gestures he made to bring her closer, he was treading on thin ice. He could literally navigate his way on thin ice—he'd been to the South Pole with explorer and entrepreneur Jefferson Haldon eighteen months ago—but this was different.

And personal relationships had always been harder for him. Give him a physical obstacle and tell him it was impossible and he'd find a way to conquer it. But give him a woman and tell him that she was impossible and he was stymied. It was frustrating to think he'd come such a long way from Frisco, Texas, and still hadn't figured women out.

This woman. Frankly, she was the only one he really wanted to unravel and strip bare. But every time he thought he had a handle on her she did something unexpected…like the squeaky voice thing. What did it mean?

Why was this making her vulnerable? He was the one putting himself on the line…or was he the only one?

"Willow, I'm being honest. There is something about you that intrigues me. Even when you're giving me the cold shoulder."

"I'd put that down to ego," she said.

"Me, too," he admitted. "I'm not used to being ignored."

"Then you don't know for sure that you like me," she said.

He crossed his arms over his chest, wondering if honesty was the key to this woman. Honesty was tricky because the truth wasn't always as nice and pretty as people wanted it to be. "Want to know a secret?"

"Sure," she said.

But there was a guarded look in her eyes, as if she was expecting him to say something…hurtful? He couldn't read it. Never had been able to. The flashes he had of her from high school were just those big eyes of hers and that guarded expression on her face.

"I'm not sure if I like myself."

Dammit, where had those words come from? He had meant to feed her some line about how she couldn't expect him to like her if she kept him from truly knowing her. What he couldn't tell her is that he'd lost the ability to care about anything but a challenge a long time ago.

"I didn't expect you to be that honest," she said. "What's not to like about you? You're charming—"

"I didn't think you'd noticed," he said, flashing her a calculated grin because he needed to get them back on familiar footing instead of staying here where he felt so damned vulnerable.

"It's hard not to when you are wooing everyone in sight."

"That's my job. I can't be successful if no one wants to talk to me. I'm the host."

"You're right about that," she said, tucking a strand of hair behind her ear. "So it's just for show?"

He shrugged. "I genuinely like talking to people and hearing their stories. They fascinate me."

That hadn't always been the case. There had been a time in his life when he'd been so focused on himself he didn't know others even existed. But his accident and hitting rock bottom had changed that. He'd needed people and had been amazed at how many had reached out to help him.

"Me, too. As long as they are moving toward helping me finish whatever I'm working on," Willow said. She was driven, and he could respect that.

"Is work all you ever think about?" he asked. She had always struck him as a workaholic. Then again, he only saw her in the context of the set, so he thought he might have it wrong. Now he wasn't so sure.

She shook her head, but then grimaced. "It is. Even when I'm out with my friends I'm always thinking of my next project. But you know how it is in our business. If you take a break for a second someone will pass you by and that's it. No one remembers your name."

"You can take a small break. How about when I get back to the East Coast you play hooky for one day?" he suggested. He needed to have her to himself so he could see if she was worth all the crazy she brought to his life.

"Why?" she asked.

"Because I want to give you something you can't give yourself." He wanted to get her to notice him, and charm and expensive gifts weren't the key to Willow. He could see that now.

"I don't know that I want that kind of gift," she said.

"Too bad. That's what I'm claiming as my favor."

"Uh, you already had your favor and it was a smokin'-hot kiss."

"Dang, that's right. Okay, fine, we'll wait until after our date or better yet, I'll make our date a no-talking-about-work one."

"If that's what you want," she said, nibbling her lower lip.

"I really should be going," she said.

But she made no move toward the door. She seemed as reluctant as he was to see this night end. "We didn't get to really enjoy our coffee since we had that little work crisis to attend to…want another cup?"

She shook her head. "Thank you, but no. I can't or I'll be up all night."

"How about seeing where that kiss could lead?" he asked.

"I want to say yes. I think that's why I'm still here. But I don't get why I'm attracted to you," she said. "It would have been so much nicer if your kiss tasted gross."

That startled a laugh out of him and he shook his head. "You really are one of a kind. Sorry for not being gross."

She gave him a really tender half smile that let him see how vulnerable she could be. And it was odd to see that expression on her face because she was always in charge. Always so in control of herself and her surroundings, but now he had a glimpse of a different side of her.

"It just makes everything so much more complicated."

"Surely you've had that happen before," he said. He couldn't believe she'd get to thirty and not have found a man she could like kissing. "Dating is never as simple as we want it to be."

"I don't really date," she admitted. "As you noted earlier I'm pretty much always all about work."

"No man asks you out?"

"They do but I'm busy and no one has intrigued me enough—"

"Enough? Enough to what?"

She tipped her head to the side, studying him with that clear cool gaze of hers. "To risk getting hurt."

"Not every relationship equals hurt," he said.

"I don't want to talk about this," she said, turning on her heel and heading toward the door.

"Who hurt you?" he asked. "Was it a lover or your father?"

She glanced back over her shoulder. "It doesn't really matter. At least not now."

Willow was surprised by how intuitive Jack was and she didn't necessarily like it. A fun bet with Nic was one thing; actually letting Jack past her defenses was something else. She'd meant it when she'd said she wished he wasn't a good kisser. She didn't want to like him.

She understood why Nichole had wanted her to come on this date. But Willow hadn't realized how much she had hidden away from her past until now. The emotions she'd thought she'd forgotten were all there stirring inside of her and making her say and do things that her common sense said not to.

"I think it does matter," he said. "I don't want to fight a ghost of a man. Tell me the details so I know what I'm up against."

No way. She didn't want to get all deep and Greek tragedy on him. She always thought of her epic quest for vengeance as some sort of ancient tale. It made it easier to wait for opportunities to strike back at Jack. Vengeance wasn't an instant gratification process.

"This was our first date," she said. "You are supposed to be thinking about asking me out on a second date, not about the other men I've dated."

"I am thinking about that, Wills, but I know that you're not going to fall for a man you can't trust. And so far all I've done to impress you is not kiss gross."

"The not being gross thing counts for a lot more than you think it does," she said, trying to move the conversation back into safer waters without letting him see how desperately she wanted to stop talking about this.

"Trust me, I'm flattered. But one of the things I'm seeing about you is that it takes more than a kiss to woo you."

"Why woo me? Can't you just do whatever it is you usually do?" she asked.

"No way. That's the surefire way to have you for just one night," he said.

That had to be a line.

"You want more than that?" she asked. "You don't even know me."

"Agreed. But I want to know you. Every time I'm with you I want to stay in your presence as long as I can. I know it's not cool to admit but I'm obsessed with you."

"Obsessed with me? As soon as you figure out why you'll move on," she said.

He shrugged. "I don't think so. That's why I need to know more about you."

She doubted that knowledge would help. But the fact that he admitted to being enamored with her was a mark in her favor. She wanted revenge and she saw that it could be very easily had if she played her cards right. Except that she was conflicted. She liked Jack.

He had a self-effacing side—something that she'd take over ego and arrogance any day. He was funny and charming and then there were his kisses, which had almost made her want to drag him to the floor and have her way with him.

"I guess next Saturday will be a big date for us, then," she said.

"Unless you want to stay here now and talk all night," he said. "I'm flying to L.A. in the morning so I don't mind."

"Really? Don't you need sleep like the rest of us?"

"I do," he said, "but for you, I'd give it up."

She had to work tomorrow but she was honest enough to admit to herself that she probably wouldn't get much sleep tonight for thinking about him. But staying here had mistake written all over it and she was done making mistakes with Jack Crown…really, she was.

"I can't. I'm not ready to be that intense with you, Jack. I'm still not sure you aren't playing some kind of game with me."

He looked hurt for a nanosecond and then covered it with a shrug. "I'm not really a player."

"Maybe not, but I don't know you well enough yet. Thanks again for helping out with Deidre, though."

"No problem. I like being able to help."

"I can see that," she said.

She reached for the doorknob and then glanced back over her shoulder to say goodbye. There was a wistful look on Jack's face. She realized then that Nichole might have known that Jack seemed to genuinely care about her. Willow didn't understand him herself. How could someone who'd treated her so callously in high school have grown into this man?

"Night," he said, lifting one hand to wave goodbye to her.

"Night," she said, walking out into the hallway and closing the door. She leaned back against it and took a deep breath. She really didn't know what had happened but her heart was racing and she regretted leaving him.

She wasn't being careful with her own emotions. Why was it that Jack Crown seemed to know the things to do and say to make her feel this way? Why couldn't she meet another man who had this kind of power over her?

Why him?

She pushed away from the door and walked down the hallway before realizing she'd forgotten her coat. Dammit, if it weren't so cold she'd just leave it. But it had been snowing when she'd arrived. She turned back and knocked on his door.

He opened it and held out her coat. She saw that he'd put his own on and had his keys in his hands. He had a scarf draped around his neck.

"I was coming after you," he said. The light from the hallway shone down on his hair and brought out the angles of his face. He was truly a very beautiful man and a part of her was angry at him just for being so damned attractive to her. Life would be much easier if he weren't. "You're going to need this."

She nodded and reached out for her coat but he held it up for her.

"Turn around," he said. "I'll help you."

She did as he asked, sliding her arms into her coat. It had been a long time since anyone had helped her with her coat and the little gesture touched her. Made her remember the other caring things he'd done tonight.

If he was playing her… He had to be playing her, didn't he?

He lifted her hair from the back of her neck where it had gotten trapped between her body and her coat.

"Damn," he said under his breath.

"What?"

"Nothing. It's just that I had a bet with myself that your hair wouldn't be as soft as it looks."

"And?"

"It's softer," he said.

He dropped her hair and then turned and went back into his apartment. All she could do was stand there feeling more confused and alone than she had in a long, long time.

Four

Peter Mullen was whipcord lean and had a grin that made you want to smile back at him. He wasn't overly tall but then he was a race car driver. And the cockpits of those things weren't made for giants.

"Do you know what Deirdre just said to me?" Kat said, coming up next to Willow where they'd set up their shot for the day. They were indoors at a charity event for the Children's Diabetes Foundation. Peter was a major sponsor.

"What?"

"She said, 'I still don't get racing. I mean, they just drive around the track. What's the point?'"

"What did you say to her?"

"That I grew up in the South. You know all we have down there is racing…go-carts, dirt bikes, you name it, guys race it," she said with a grin.

Willow had to laugh at Kat. The woman was five

years younger than her but they had the same sensibility. It was one of the reasons why Willow had hired her. She'd been grooming Kat—well, mentoring her would be a better way of putting it.

"You're kidding me," Willow said. It seemed as though Deidre was determined to not make the match with Peter work. A part of Willow wondered why she'd even gone to a matchmaker but she knew the other woman must have had a good reason.

"Do you think I should go and explain it to her?" Willow asked. She wasn't too sure she could explain racing, having not really watched it herself.

"No. I already gave her an iPad loaded with the information. Told her if Peter could read all her columns the least she could do was understand what he did for a living," Kat said.

Uh-oh. Kat had a way of shooting from the hip sometimes. "Did you say it like that?"

"What, am I stupid?" Kat said. "Of course not. But I wanted to. Why did she even go to a matchmaker?"

"I don't know. I'll go talk to her," Willow said. She understood being reluctant—after all, everybody had their share of battle scars when it came to relationships and love. But Deidre had sought this out.

"Fine by me. I'll go talk to Peter," Kat said.

Willow had the feeling that Kat liked Peter more than just as a friend. Every time they were together on set Kat was over there batting her eyelashes and flirting with him. "He's spoken for."

"I know that," the other woman said.

"Just make sure you remember it," Willow said before walking away. She had a radio on her belt and an earpiece in her ear so she could hear whatever a craft or services person needed from her as they prepared to shoot the episode.

Peter and Deidre were the last couple featured in this first season of *Sexy & Single.* Willow just wanted them to make a spectacular ending to her show so that advertisers would come back and viewers would keep tuning in.

She walked into the large bathroom that they had commandeered as a dressing room/greenroom for the day. Deidre was sitting in front of a bank of mirrors alone. She seemed small and like someone who didn't know everything in that moment. Willow cleared her throat and as instantaneously as a switch being thrown, Deidre changed.

Suddenly she looked like Ms. D, the advice columnist famous for her tough love approach to problems. But Willow had seen the woman behind the curtain and for the first time since Deidre had come on the show, Willow felt a bit of sympathy toward her.

"Hello," Willow said. "How's it going?"

Deidre turned to face her, that clear gray gaze of hers cutting past the niceties that Willow's Texas mom had drilled into her. "I'm not going to be difficult. I've spoken to Mona and to Jack. I know what you need from me."

Willow shook her head. "There is no one here but you and me, Deidre. No audience listening in, no one who is going to judge you. Just another woman who has had her own dating problems and I'm asking you woman-to-woman if you're okay."

Deidre stared at her for a long minute and then she shook her head. "I'm not sure what I expected from matchmaking…but I don't like Peter."

"What don't you like?" Willow said.

"He's too…" She looked down at her lap where her hands were clenched together.

"Too?"

"Too much. He makes me face things that I don't want to. I wanted a man who'd just be a companion, but he wants more."

In that moment Willow totally understood Deidre. "I get it. Are you attracted to him?"

"Yes. But I can't figure out why. He's so not the man I would have picked for myself," Deidre said.

"That's probably precisely why. Mona has a way of seeing past all the things that you think you want and finding someone who really can complete you."

"How do you know? Have you been to her?" Deidre asked, that unflinching gray gaze of hers focused on Willow. It made her uncomfortable.

"No. But one of my best friends has. Gail Little was matched with someone who she thought was her polar opposite but she was wrong. I'm not saying it was easy for her, but you have to give Peter a chance. Give Mona a chance."

"I already said I would," Deidre said. The fragility she'd been exhibiting just a moment earlier was gone.

"You said it, but you are just going through the motions. You have to really let Peter in or you won't know if he's right for you or not."

"I know," Deidre said. "You're not saying anything to me that I haven't said to my own readers. But it's easier to tell someone else to take a chance than it is to take a chance myself. I just don't know if I can do it."

"Nothing hurts worse than a broken heart," Willow said, speaking from that place herself. That was precisely why she was dithering when it came to Jack. If she could believe he was a charming rogue she could do what needed to be done—get her revenge and walk away. But he was so much more than that.

"Exactly. And do you see the way he moves, the way he smiles... I'm just so afraid that I'm going to fall for him as he speeds through my life and on to the next adventure."

Deidre had just summed up what Willow herself had felt the other night at Jack's. Of course, it was easier for Willow to encourage Deidre to give Peter a chance to prove her wrong because as Deidre had said, giving advice was so much easier than taking it.

"It's just six dates," Willow said. "Actually only five more dates since you've already had your first one."

Deidre gave her a smile that was so full of fear that Willow wanted to give the other woman a hug. "Six dates is going to be just long enough for me to fall in love with him."

"You think so?"

She nodded. "That's why I'm so afraid to keep doing this."

"But you're going to, right?"

"I have to. If I back out now I'm never going to take a chance like this again," she said, then gave a very wry laugh. "It's Peter or no one for me."

"Why did you sign up for the matchmaking?" Willow asked. "Don't take this the wrong way but you don't seem like you're that open to sharing your life."

"That's precisely why. Do you know how I spend most of my days?"

"No."

"Alone with my cats, doling out advice to people who...well, people who are out there living their lives. I spent my summer vacation in an old folks' home with my great-aunt and took a look around me. That is the path I am headed down if I don't get out of this rut. No matter how much Peter scares me I don't want to be like Auntie Randi."

Those words echoed in Willow's head for the rest of the day. She was hoping that she'd be able to tip the scales of heartbreak with Jack by finding another man. But was she just fooling herself? Usually she didn't think about the future because she was grounded in the now and guided by the past. But she had an image of herself in a home all alone and frankly that scared her even more than risking herself with Jack.

"So am I getting an all-expenses-paid trip to the Red Door Spa or what?" Nichole asked as she slid into the booth next to Willow. Gail was already sliding in on the other side trapping her in the middle.

They were in a banquette booth at China Fun, a place that had been recommended to Nichole by one of her coworkers at *America Today.*

"Not yet," Willow said. "The food better be good here."

"I know Chinese isn't your favorite but I've been craving it and Conner said he can't do any more dim sum," Nichole said, rubbing her belly.

"You owe me," Willow said.

"Me, too," Gail said. "Russell wanted to tag along but since Nichole had mentioned the bet, I made him stay home. I need details."

The waiter saved Willow from having to spill just yet as he came by to take their drink order. But as soon as he left, both women turned to look at her, and she wanted to sink back into the cushions and disappear.

There was a reason why she produced and directed television shows—she didn't like having any attention directed at her. But these women were her best buds. She needed to talk but just had no idea what to say.

"Jack isn't a complete douche," she said at last. She was a little bit angry at herself for not being able to just hate him.

Gail, who had been taking a sip of water, laughed and almost choked on it. "Oh, my God. Don't do that when I'm drinking."

"Sorry," Willow said. And she was. Being a brat wasn't her usual mode of operation. It was just that after the long day on the set with Deidre and Peter and the gloomy image she had of her future, she was unsure. And she hated not knowing what to do.

"I just don't know what to say," she said at last.

"That was a great start," Nichole said. "But we already knew that—or at least I did. Have you talked to him much, Gail?"

"Not really—just when I was on the show. So you went to his place, Will. What was it like?" Gail asked. Her friend wore her shoulder-length hair down. She had on horn-rimmed glasses but her brilliant brown eyes were still visible. Gail looked happy, which made Willow feel good because she'd had a part in that by helping Gail get through a tough patch with Russell Holloway.

"Comfortable. He had his housekeeper cook dinner for us," Willow said. She reran the night in her head. How was she going to explain that kiss? If she wasn't comfortable thinking about it how could she possibly talk about it with her friends?

"Nice. What else?"

"He had a Beckendorf hanging on his wall…"

"Ah, see, it's Fate. I'm glad I stopped you from chickening out," Nichole said, waving over the waiter. "Sorry, ladies, but I'm starving. Can we order?"

Willow nodded. Anything that kept them from talking about her date with Jack was preferable. How could it be Fate with Jack? Karma, she could understand, but that was it. There was nothing truly remarkable about the fact that they both supported a Texas artist.

Her iPhone buzzed in her pocket and she pulled it out to check her messages. Usually it was a Twitter or Facebook alert but this time it was a text message from Jack with a photo of himself under a billboard on the corner of Sunset Boulevard. The ad was for *Sexy & Single.* The message he'd typed said Next stop: Emmy.

She laughed. He got it. Actually, he got her. He knew that for her the show was the most important thing in her life.

"What is it?" Gail asked, leaning over her shoulder.

"That's so cute," Nichole said. "I'm going to the salon on your dime."

She shook her head. "You haven't won yet. He's charming and he knows it."

"Of course he does. My mom would have said God smiled on him and she'd have been right. Are you going to text him back?" Gail said.

"Not while you two are staring over my shoulder," Willow said. She didn't mind sharing things with her best friends but this thing with Jack…well, she just really didn't know how to handle it and she didn't want witnesses if she fell on her face.

"Fine. I have to go to the bathroom," Nichole said. "Gail, come with me so I don't accidently fall."

"This pregnancy thing is going to your head. You're not a princess, you know," Gail said, grumbling as she slid out of the booth to follow her friend.

"Yes, I am."

The women kept up their friendly banter as they

moved out of earshot and Willow just stared down at her phone and that goofy picture of Jack. He was smiling and making a thumbs-up sign. She'd never have the confidence to send him a picture like that.

But then she shook her head. Why not? She had nothing to lose, this was her chance to heal and move on. And Jack seemed to be open and honest with her.

But that was the way he'd seemed all those years ago. Had she really learned nothing from her heartbreak? Sure, he seemed fun and like a guy she'd want to date, but that was his agenda. And hers was revenge. It didn't matter how "nice" he seemed, he hadn't proven to her that he'd changed.

Even so, she picked up her wineglass and held out her cell phone to snap a picture of herself. She typed in the message Drinks are on me at the Emmy after party if we make it.

She hit Send before she had second thoughts and then put her phone back in her pocket. Jack was messing with her head and making her act like…like she'd never had her heart broken. She supposed that was a good thing.

She knew she'd let a lot of good men slip away over the years because she'd been afraid to relax and be herself. With Jack…she should be doubly wary, she thought.

"Did you send your message?" Gail asked as she sat back down.

"Yes, where's Nic?"

"Talking to Conner now. I needed… Don't tell her but I'm having a hard time with her being pregnant."

Willow put her arm around Gail's shoulders. Gail had wanted a family of her own, which was the main reason why she'd gone to Matchmakers, Inc. to find a husband. It had only been after she and Russell had started dating that she'd learned he was sterile and couldn't have kids.

It had been a blow for Gail and a bit of a shock for Willow to learn since Russell had been settling paternity suits with ex-girlfriends for years. He'd done it mainly to help out the women but also because he hadn't wanted the world to know that he couldn't have kids of his own. He'd had a reputation to keep up; for Russell, the ability to procreate had been tied to his own masculinity, and he hadn't wanted the world to know he couldn't have kids.

"I'm sorry."

"Don't be. I've got a great man and a good life. It's just that sometimes I'm envious."

"Me, too. Nic makes everything seem so easy," Willow said.

"Who makes everything seem easy?" Nichole said as she sat back down.

"You," Willow said.

"As if. I'm a mess and you both know it. I can't have caffeine while I'm pregnant, my feet are swollen and though he denies it, I'm sure Conner wishes I wasn't as big as I am."

"Oh, my, it's so funny how on the outside it seems no one has any problems."

"But we all do," Gail said.

Everyone did have problems, Willow thought. Did Jack? If so, what was he hiding? And if not, she needed to know the answer soon so she could get some closure from the past.

Willow was surprised when she arrived at work the next morning and found a FedEx package waiting for her. Her offices in Midtown often received shipments but this was the first time she'd had one from Jack. She opened the medium box expecting…hell, she didn't know what she was expecting because he shouldn't have been sending her anything. She tipped the box over on her desk and three small wrapped boxes fell to the surface.

She sat down in her chair and leaned back in it, studying the gifts. Why was Jack sending her gifts? Damn, this was way more complicated than she'd expected. Yet it wasn't. She felt a thrill deep in her stomach as she reached for the first gift without thinking and started opening the paper. But then she noticed a small note underneath the presents.

She pulled the note toward herself and saw her name printed in Jack's bold style. She recognized the handwriting immediately as it hadn't changed since high school. She traced her finger over the letters of her own name then opened the note.

Willow,

I saw these and thought of you. I hope you like them. Can't wait for our date on Saturday.

Jack.

She put the note aside, lifting up the first package which was a rectangular box. She unwrapped it slowly then felt silly—it wasn't as if he'd sent her a bomb. Another little note was taped to the brown box.

A hug that won't get your back up.

She carefully opened the box and pulled out the small knickknack. It was a figurine of two bears hugging each other. The bigger bear had eyes the same color as Jack's. She ran her fingers over the little statuette, taking a moment to put the paper in the trash can and set the note underneath the bears. She moved it over next to her phone so she could see it but anyone entering her office wouldn't be able to.

She set it aside and reached for the next present. She didn't think about the emotions that were roiling through her at that moment because she wasn't ready to deal with them.

The second present was also in a little brown box and when she pulled it out and peeled away the bubble wrap she saw it was a frog prince with a crown on it…a tiny trinket box. There was a hinge under the pillow the frog was sitting on where the box opened up to reveal another note.

Even I know that I'm still a prince in frog's clothing.

She swallowed hard as tears burned the back of her eyes. How did Jack know the exact right things to say to her? Could one dinner with him have really laid all of her soul bare? She knew it hadn't. Knew that she'd said he was charming in that sarcastic way of hers and this is how he'd interpreted it.

A cold knot inside her heart where she'd dreamed of revenge against Jack Crown was starting to melt. And frankly that scared her.

Scared her because he was making her care about him and even worse than that he was making her believe he might really care for her. She was almost afraid to open the last box but when she did she found a set of six wineglass charms that reminded her of Texas, as they included three cowboy boots in red, white and blue and three cowboy hats in different colors.

To remind you of our shared past.

She shook her head and pushed back from her desk, walking away from the gifts that Jack had sent her. He'd done a good job of finding just the right things to speak to her soul, but that last one—the reminder of their shared past—was the one that was causing her the most conflict.

She didn't want to remember the old Jack and yet she knew that boy was part of the man he was today.

She didn't want to trust that boy. She'd done so once at her own peril.

"Hey, boss lady. You ready for an exciting day of love in the big city?" Kat asked as she entered the main office area. Kat had on one of those goofy hats shaped like an animal head that they sold to tourists in Times Square. Her coat was an old navy peacoat that Kat had inherited from her grandfather when he'd died.

"Always. That's why I'm so successful," Willow said. And to be honest, she needed work today to get her mind off Jack.

"That and coffee," Kat said, pulling her hands from behind her back and showing off two Starbucks cups. "I'm the best assistant in the world."

"Yes, you are," Willow said, getting up from her desk and walking over to Kat. But as they reviewed the footage from the day before and she made notes for the editor, she couldn't help but think of the little gifts sitting on her desk.

That frog was so Jack. Pretty and pompous and full of the self-deprecating humor that made him so different from the boy she'd known long ago. Nichole had been wiser than Willow had given her credit for when she'd suggested that Jack was the key to unlocking something inside of her. She hadn't realized how much she'd given up when she'd let Jack's attitude twist the way she looked at men.

And those gifts from him were showing her how much she'd missed out on. She'd rarely let any man see a part of her that she'd shown Jack the other night. Was she awakening to a new self or was it Jack who was responsible?

"Willow?"

"Yes?"

"Phone's for you," Kat said. "It's Jack."

"I'll take it in my office," Willow said, heading back to her office and closing the door behind her. She sat down and reached for the phone.

"This is Willow."

"Good morning. Did you get my package?" Jack asked.

His deep husky voice brushed over her senses, leaving a tingling trail in its wake. She rubbed her hands over her arms and closed her eyes, remembering the last time he'd spoken to her in the hallway outside his apartment. She had wished a hundred times she'd gone back in there and had sex with him. Then she could have walked away the next morning and kept her emotions safely buttoned up.

Instead she'd opened herself up to dating and already she knew that was a mistake. The gifts, the texts and now this morning call were all signs that they were getting in too deep.

"I did...why are you calling me so early? Shouldn't you still be in bed?" she asked. It was nine on the East Coast, which meant it was only six in Los Angeles.

"Got a shoot this morning with PJ Montaine...surfing in Malibu."

"You do lead a hard life," Willow said. She wasn't ready to talk to Jack about anything consequential. She needed time and privacy and she hoped that there would be enough of both before she saw him again so she could figure out exactly what she needed.

Silence buzzed on the line and she looked for something to say so she could end this call.

"Did you like my gifts?" he asked.

"Yes. They were fun and made me smile. Thank you," she said.

"You're welcome. I saw them in the lobby gift shop and since I was thinking of you—"

"Were you thinking of me?" she asked.

"All the time," he said with a sigh she heard through the phone. "I can't wait to see you again. What about you?"

She took a deep breath. "I've been thinking of you, too. You are without a doubt the most complicated man I've ever met."

"You sound frustrated."

"I am."

"Sexually?"

Startled, she had to laugh. "A little bit. This would be a lot easier if it was just about sex. Is it for you?"

Five

Sex. She wanted to know if he was pursuing her just for sex. It had started out that way; he wasn't going to lie about that to himself. But he'd dated enough women to know he could never say that out loud.

In his mind he knew the exact moment when Willow became a woman he wanted in his bed as opposed to being a girl he used to know that he worked with now. And though he'd spent a lot of time imagining her straddling his lap with that long fall of black hair spilling over her shoulders as she rode him, that wasn't what had made the crucial difference in how he'd seen her.

No, that had been an unexpected moment when he'd been on the set with the second couple on the show—Alex Cannon and Fiona McCaw. Fiona had her sweet little daughter, Bella Ann, with her.

Seeing Willow holding Fiona's baby had been like a bolt of lightning to him. He caught a glimpse behind that prickly shield of hers and something had changed. He'd seen a bit of longing and such adoration for that baby that he wanted to pull her into his arms and promise her that he'd give her whatever she wanted.

"Jack?" she asked.

"Yeah?" he answered, still stuck somewhere in the past and in a fantasy where they didn't have all the pressures of his job and lifestyle. Not to mention her job and her hang-up when it came to men and dating.

"So it is all about sex for you?" she asked. He heard more than just a tinge of disappointment in her voice. And though he knew he shouldn't be, he was upset that she'd been so easily let down by him.

"I should have guessed," she said at last.

"Don't put words in my mouth, Willow. Of course I want you. You're one sexy woman and when I'm with you I can't help thinking about what it would be like to have those long legs of yours wrapped around my hips."

"Really?" she asked, that adorable little squeak of hers making an appearance.

"Yes," he said because he couldn't think of Willow and not think about having her in his arms. "But it's not just that. I also think about how your silky hair will feel against my chest when I hold you afterward, but that doesn't mean I just want sex from you."

"Why not?" she asked. "If this was just a one-night thing we could both just do it and move on."

"I don't know," he said and he meant it. He was the king of moving on but he didn't want to fly through Willow's life. He wanted more. "There is something about you that keeps me coming back for more. Even when you're giving me the cold shoulder, you're the only woman I want."

"Is it because of that?" she asked. "Maybe I seem unattainable, so you want to prove you can get me."

"No. I know this will come as a shock to you but women have said no to me before." He'd already run over that scenario in his head. Maybe when he'd first shown up on set the challenge of overcoming Willow's resistance had been his motivation but once he'd seen her with that baby everything had changed.

He didn't want to believe that he'd changed. Wouldn't admit that maybe he wanted something more from life than his solo run through it. But a part of him sort of did.

"I never thought you'd admit that out loud," she said wryly.

"Well, I don't want you to get the wrong impression of me," he said. Usually he didn't care what people thought of him. He knew that most thought he'd had more than his share of good luck directed his way, but none of those strangers understood the cost of being that lucky. No one else got that dreams had to die for his golden opportunities to show up. And he didn't want Willow to be another dead dream from his past.

"What impression should I get?" she asked.

He wished he could see her face so he'd know what she wanted from him. He didn't like this feeling. It was almost like when he'd woken up in the hospital after that game-ending injury. He'd had no idea what he wanted to do with his life or what direction to go in.

Right now he knew he could say the wrong thing and that Willow would drift farther away from him.

But he also knew he could say the right thing and bring her closer. And wasn't that the fly in the ointment? He'd never known the right words for any woman and especially not with Willow.

What were the right words? He had no idea. He was

just a guy who was used to dating in a shallow world and Willow, despite the fact that she'd been dating in the same world, expected something more from the men in her life. There was a reason she was still single and he had the distinct feeling it was because her standards were high.

He settled for something halfway between the truth and a line. "Just that I'm a guy who wants to make a good impression on you. I don't want you to lump me together with every other guy you've cared about, but didn't end up with."

"How do you know that I've cared about another guy?" she asked and there was more than a hint of weariness in her tone now.

She made it impossible to ever really get closer to her because every time he thought he had her figured out something else came up.

"Because you're not a teenager anymore and no one gets to our age without experiencing heartbreak at least once," Jack said. That was one thing he'd learned—that fame had no influence over. Some of his most famous celebrity friends had been hurt worse than the average Joes he met when he was out doing a promo tour.

"Even the ever-charming Jack Crown?" she asked.

He noted that she didn't deny the heartbreak and made a mental note to find out more about that. She was very good about changing the subject back to him.

"I thought my gift made it clear…I'm still in my frog's clothing," he said because most of his heartbreak hadn't been interpersonal but had involved big life-changing events.

"Waiting for the right kiss?" she asked.

"I think I might have had the right kiss the other

night. Just not enough of them," he said, trying to lighten his own mood. "I definitely think you should try again."

"Oh, you. If I believed even half the stuff that came out of your mouth I'd be in trouble."

He didn't know how to take that. "This isn't a game for me."

"Isn't it?"

"No. If I was interested in that type of thing I wouldn't try to pursue you while I'm taping two shows and flying between coasts each week. The timing isn't right."

"Then why are you pursuing me?"

"Because you finally said yes," Jack said. "That's all I really know, Willow."

"Things like that make it hard to keep doubting you," she said at last. "And I don't want to like you."

"Why is that?" he asked.

"It has to do with high school," she said. "But I don't want to talk about it on the phone."

"Okay. We can chat about the past on Saturday. Did I do something wrong back then?"

"Don't you remember?" she asked.

He didn't. He'd always made it a policy to not look back. He was sure part of it had to do with losing his father at a very young age and then always having to move around with his single mother as she tried to keep a job. "Not really. I try to keep facing forward."

"I can't do that," she said. "Everything in our pasts defines where we are today."

"But you have to let go of that to move on," Jack said. "Is that why you didn't want to go out with me?"

"Yes," she said. "The boy you were—never mind. We can talk about that later."

He didn't want to let it go but he also wanted to see her face when they discussed the past. What had he done? He honestly didn't remember anything upsetting happening during those years. He'd spent so much time on the football field, focused on getting a full-ride scholarship so his mom wouldn't have to worry about putting him through college.

"Okay. I was really just calling to make sure you'd gotten my gifts."

"I did. Thank you again."

"You're very welcome," he said. "Have a good day."

"You, too," she said.

He hung up the phone and lay back on his bed. Though he'd known that the path to Willow was going to be complicated he hadn't expected this. What had he done to her in the past? Was it something that he could make right now?

It was colder than normal for November, even though it was Southern California. But the surf at Malibu was good this time of year, and championship surfer PJ Montaine was in one of his gregarious moods, talking to the crew as the cameraman mounted the camera to a surf board so they could tape every second while they were out in the Pacific Ocean.

PJ's job as a professional surfer was the subject of this episode of *Extreme Careers,* which was the show Jack liked best of all the ones he hosted.

Jack had surfed for the first time when he'd come to L.A. to start working in TV, and PJ had been the one to teach him. The same sports agent, Gary Horowitz, had represented them both back then.

"I hear you're working on a matchmaking show… thinking of settling down?" PJ asked as they took a break from filming and got into their wet suits.

He thought about Willow and how much he wanted

her in his bed, but that was sex and not love. Jack wasn't sure marriage was for him. After all, someone had to believe in forever to make that kind of commitment. And he had lost that belief a long time ago.

"Nah, it's just a way to make a living."

"Do you like it?" PJ asked.

"I do. It's fun to talk to the couples as they try to figure out if what they wanted when they went to the matchmaker is actually coming true or if they've made a huge mistake. It's wicked complicated," Jack said.

"Understatement of the year, man. I remember when Rhia and I first started dating. Hell, I didn't think I'd ever feel confident that she was my woman. Dating is so tumultuous. I bet it makes for some great episodes on the show."

"Yes, it does," Jack said. But his mind was on Willow. Tumultuous pretty much summed her up and how he felt about her. She had been stonewalling him since May when he'd first been brought to *Sexy & Single* and started asking her out.

For his part, he wanted her. She was slim and sexy and had this way of looking at him that frankly made him hard. There was something about a woman in control that turned him on. But with Willow it was more than sex. He wanted to unravel all her secrets and find out why she was such a badass now. The girl he remembered from Texas hadn't been.

"Ready to do this?" the director, Ben Johnson, said, coming over to him.

Jack glanced at the waves and then over at PJ and nodded. The sooner they got this session taped and edited the sooner he could head back to the East Coast. Though given Willow's reaction to the presents he'd sent her this morning, he'd say his wooing was going better with the distance between them.

He chalked that up to her orneriness. Every other woman he'd dated had wanted to spend time going out to the A-list restaurants and nightclubs so they could be seen. Willow seemed to prefer eating in his apartment and getting gifts from him when he was gone.

"Crazy."

"What is?" PJ asked as he walked over to him.

"Women," Jack said.

PJ laughed. "You can say that again. You ready to do this?"

"Yes," Jack said. They both grabbed their boards and waded out into the ocean. Jack listened to Ben's directions and then got on his board to paddle out beyond the breaks. The water was cold, even though he had the wet suit on. He wondered if Willow had ever been surfing. Would she enjoy it? He knew he'd like to see her in a bikini.

"I'll take the first set," PJ said.

Jack nodded and watched his friend paddling toward the wave. Jack saw something swimming in the water near PJ and wondered if it was the school of dolphins that they'd seen earlier. He'd taped his intro with the porpoises frolicking behind him.

But then he saw the dorsal fin at the same moment that PJ screamed and fell into the water. There was thrashing and Jack stopped thinking, realizing that PJ was being attacked by a shark.

He dove into the water, trying to remember the advice he'd read on shark attacks. He thought attacking them, punching them in the nose, would get them to loosen up. Jack drew back his fist and hit the shark as hard as he could, not once but three times in a row. There was so much blood he could scarcely see through it but he managed to grab PJ as the lifeguard/medic who was on the shoot swam out to them. Together they got PJ free and swam with him to shore.

Jack couldn't stop shaking as the medic went to work on PJ. But his friend was unresponsive as he was loaded onto the ambulance.

"I'm going with him," Jack said, getting into the back of the ambulance with the medic.

No one argued.

The director yelled that he'd meet him at the hospital and Jack couldn't say anything. He'd had brushes with death before but this one…this one had scared the hell out of him. He couldn't believe that PJ was lying there practically lifeless after just joking and laughing what seemed like seconds earlier.

Dammit, Jack thought. This was why…

"You okay, man?" the medic asked.

"Yeah. Is he going to make it?"

"I don't know. He lost a lot of blood, but I've got him stabilized. That was some quick thinking jumping on the shark the way you did. How'd you know to do that?"

"I didn't. I just knew I had to do something. I wasn't really thinking."

"Well, you've got good instincts. If he makes it, it will be thanks to you."

God, please let him make it, Jack prayed to himself. He'd never been overly religious despite his mother's best efforts. But he reached out all the same. He needed to believe there was someone up there listening who could help his friend pull through.

PJ was finally settling down to live the good life. He'd just gotten married to a television actress and Jack wanted to believe his friend could have it all. He wanted to believe that he could have it all, too, but this incident made him realize that no one was guaranteed anything.

There could be no more slow and gentle wooing of Willow. Time might not be on his side. An accident could end things at any moment and every opportunity that he'd missed would turn to regret.

Willow tried not to think about her latest conversation with Jack and did a pretty good job of ignoring it until she got home and climbed into bed just before midnight. She knew it was her own fault for putting that stupid frog prince on her nightstand. And then, because she knew no one else would ever know, she'd kissed it.

She'd closed her eyes and imagined the frog turning into Jack—and she'd wanted that so much that she knew she'd crossed a line. It was one thing to let this new thing with Jack "heal" the wounded part of her soul; it was something else entirely to fall for him.

That wasn't part of the plan. Not now, not ever. Jack wasn't the man for her and she didn't want him to be. She needed a guy who stayed at home and worked a normal job so she could be the star in their relationship. But she wasn't looking for that with Jack. She was looking for revenge. Why, oh, why couldn't she remember that?

She turned on her side and then realized she wasn't going to be able to sleep. Not right now. So she got up and went to her big iMac computer and opened the file the editor from *Sexy & Single* had sent her. Work had been the one thing that had saved her from being lonely and scared. And there had been plenty of times when it would have been too easy to be overwhelmed by those emotions.

Even though Gail and Nichole had always lived nearby, the three of them were all very busy with their careers. And Willow had kept a part of herself locked away. She knew that Jack had wounded something inside of her all those years ago but it was a part of herself that she didn't like to admit she had.

Deidre and Peter made good television, Willow thought as she watched the rough edit. Both were used to being in charge and both wanted something from the other. And despite the fear that Deidre had admitted to Willow when they were alone, she was flirty with Peter and kept him on his toes.

What Willow saw on the screen was the kind of honest emotion that viewers latched onto. It was the kind of thing that Willow herself liked to see because when she watched Deidre taking a risk with her heart, Willow could live vicariously through her.

Disgusted with herself and her thoughts she pushed away from her desk and went to the kitchen to make herself a cup of Sleepytime Tea. Maybe that would help her calm down enough to get some rest.

But she doubted it. She could say it was work or whatever other excuse she wanted to make but the truth was she wanted Jack to be back on the East Coast so she could see him. She wanted to go to him and confront him about the past so she'd know easily if she could trust him now.

The teakettle whistled and she poured the water over her tea letting the scent of it fill the air in her kitchen. She took her cup to the couch and sat down in her favorite corner and turned on the TV. She pulled the afghan her grandmother had knitted for her when she was born around her shoulders and turned on *Hollywood Today,* instantly noticing the flashing breaking news graphic.

She turned up the volume and leaned forward. *Accident on the beach set of* Extreme Careers *today. We only know that Jack Crown and PJ Montaine were surfing and one of them didn't make it back to shore. We are going to be live from Cedars-Sinai with the latest.*

Willow stood up so quickly that she burned herself with the tea as it sloshed over the edge of her cup. Cursing, she ran to her bedroom to grab her phone from her beside table. She was cold with fear as she called Jack's number.

Had he been hurt? Was he even now being rushed to the emergency room? His phone rang and rang as she went back to the living room to watch as *Hollywood Today* cut to the outside of the hospital.

The call went to Jack's voice mail and Willow didn't know what else to do. She was scared that Jack might be hurt. Why did it matter? Just a second ago she was debating—stop it, she thought. She'd been lying to herself from the beginning. She liked Jack and she wanted him to be that prince in frog's clothing for her.

She dialed Nichole's number but hung up before it could ring. Was she really going to get her pregnant friend out of bed in the middle of the night to check the AP wire? She could do that herself. Willow got on her computer and was typing Jack's name into the search engine when her phone rang.

She glanced at the ID just in time to see it was him.

"Jack? Oh. My. God. Are you okay?"

"Yes. I'm fine. PJ is in a coma, though," Jack said.

"I'm sorry, Jack. I..." She couldn't think of anything else to say except, "I'm so glad you are okay. *Hollywood Today* didn't say who was hurt. I was so afraid it was you."

"It wasn't," he said.

"Thank God," she said. "Do they think PJ will pull through?"

"They're not sure," Jack said, his voice breaking. "I've known PJ forever. He's a friend, Willow."

She should have realized that—most of the people that Jack had on his show were his friends. "Are you okay? What happened?"

"I'm shook up, but fine. He was attacked by a shark. I've never seen anything like it," Jack said.

"What can I do?" Willow asked. Jack sounded not scared exactly but definitely shaky, and she wanted to help him if she could.

"Just hearing your voice is helping. Why did you call? I thought after our earlier conversation, well, that maybe things were going to be different between us."

"You thought wrong," she said. She wasn't going to deny there was still a lot about Jack she didn't trust but she could no longer pretend that he didn't matter to her.

Six

Jack got off the plane at JFK Airport, donned his dark sunglasses and walked quickly through the throngs of people with his head down. He was tired, worried about PJ and wanted to see Willow. But after their last conversation he hadn't wanted to ask her for anything.

He already felt too vulnerable where she was concerned. And with everything that was going through his mind right now, he knew better than to reach out to her. He'd do something stupid that he'd regret later.

Though Willow had made jokes about his fans, he did have them, and there were times like today when he was exhausted from traveling and worrying about one of his friends, that he didn't want to be "seen." He made it out of the airport and was looking for the car he'd hired when he heard someone calling his name.

He bit back a curse and then recognized the voice. He wouldn't have thought it possible but there was Willow Stead, standing a few feet from him wearing jeans and a leather jacket and looking like the total badass she could be when she put her mind to it.

"Well, hello, gorgeous," he said in his best sexy voice. She'd surprised him and he couldn't remember the last time anyone had done that. He was so damned happy to see her it was all he could do not to reach out and lift her off her feet while he hugged her.

"Hello yourself. I figured you might appreciate a friendly face when you landed," she said. "I called your agent and got your flight number."

"I do," he said, shifting his overnight bag from one shoulder to the other.

"Great," she said. "You look tired."

"I am. I just want to get someplace where I can crash," he said.

"Then follow me."

He did, pulling out his cell phone to text the car company he'd arranged to meet him and tell them he didn't need a ride. He followed Willow to the parking garage and a restored 1979 MGB with a ragtop. It wasn't the car he expected her to drive. He hadn't even expected her to have a car because she lived in New York.

The November air was chilly after the warmer Los Angeles weather, but he welcomed it because the cold air meant he was back on the same coast as Willow and he'd missed her. She opened the trunk and he tossed his carry-on bag inside, then closed the hood and turned toward her.

"Don't take this as anything more than comfort," she said, wrapping her arms around him and hugging him. "I'm sorry about what happened to your friend."

He held her close and lowered his head to breath in

the fresh scent of her hair. Since PJ's accident something had changed between them.

"Thank you," he said.

"How's he doing?" she asked, tipping her head up and looking at him.

"Still in a coma," Jack said, stepping back away from her. He didn't want to talk about PJ. Right now he was putting that entire situation in the darkest recesses of his mind. He didn't want to let Willow know that he'd been plagued with what-ifs, second-guessing himself and his response time to his friend.

She let her arms fall to her sides. "Good flight?"

He nodded as she walked around her car and opened the driver's-side door. She leaned over to unlock his door and he got in the car.

It was small and a tight fit. She glanced at him and he tried not to look scrunched up. But he had to crouch a little to keep his head from hitting the roof. He messed around with the seat until he got the back adjusted and he could sit up straight.

"I didn't think about how big you are," she said.

"Didn't you?" he asked with a wicked grin. Because he was tired, she'd hugged him and he wanted her. Finally something to distract him from the shark attack and PJ's coma.

She blushed and shook her head at him. "I knew it was all about sex with you."

"Not all," he reminded her. "Maybe you should give me another kiss and see if I turn into a prince."

She smiled over at him and he knew that she wanted him, too.

"What if it makes you more froggy?"

"That's a chance I'm willing to take."

"Of course you are," she said with a wink. "I'm the one who's kissing a frog."

He laughed at that. "Damn, I missed you."

"Me, too," she said. "I tried not to but on the set it wasn't the same without your big ego there to demand attention from everyone."

"Glad I'm unforgettable," he said.

"You can be," she admitted. "Now tell me more about everything with PJ. What happened? On the TV they just said shark attack."

He didn't really know where to begin. "Um…we were surfing and a shark attacked PJ. I was close to him, close enough to be the first responder. I hit the shark in the eyes and somehow we got PJ free."

"Are you okay?"

"You know I am. I just did what I needed to and tried to save PJ. I wonder if I could have done something better."

"No. I'm sure you did everything you could," she said.

He shrugged and looked out the window. He had no idea if there was more he could have done. He just didn't know.

"So you said he's in a coma?"

"Yes, he lost a lot of blood and they had to amputate his leg," Jack said. "But he's getting better. He responded to Rhia's voice as soon as she got to the hospital and went in to talk to him."

"That's good. So you know PJ well." she said.

"Yes. He was one of the first guys I met on the West Coast. We had the same sports agent."

"I'm sorry this happened," she said.

"I don't want to talk about it anymore," he said.

"Okay. Will you have to go back to shoot another episode?"

"No. I told the producers to find me someone on the East Coast. I'm doing a Thanksgiving Day special for one of the networks and since there are only two more weeks until then, I want to stay put," he said. He looked over at her as she drove out of the airport and negotiated the traffic toward the city. "Plus there is someone I'd like to spend a little more time with."

"I'm glad," she said. "Do you have anywhere you need to be?"

"Not right away," he said. "Why?"

"Want to have brunch with me?"

"I'd love to," he said. He knew that all this agreeableness couldn't last—it just wasn't in Willow's nature—but he was enjoying it for right now. "Don't take this the wrong way, but why are you being so nice to me?"

She stopped for traffic and glanced over at him, raising one eyebrow. "Am I usually not nice?"

"Ah, of course you are. Just not to me."

She shrugged as the cars started moving again and turned her attention to driving. "When I didn't know if you were okay I had an epiphany of sorts."

"And that was?" he asked after he realized she wasn't going to say anything else.

"It was just this feeling in my gut that I might have really missed out on something special by not getting to know you," she said.

He reached over and squeezed her shoulder, but didn't say anything. What could he really say? He felt the same way but he had no idea where this was going. And seeing how quickly fate could change a man's life…well, being reminded of how easily the plans he made could be altered by one event had brought home to him that he might have no more time with Willow than these remaining weeks on *Sexy & Single.*

And he really didn't want to waste a single one of them. He still planned to woo her and win her, but now the timetable felt even more compacted because he had been reminded that life wasn't guaranteed to be long. It could all end tomorrow and he didn't want his last thoughts to be regrets of what could have been with Willow.

He didn't pay much attention to their route, just watched Willow as she drove in the dappled morning November sun. It was clear today and seemed even colder when she pulled to a stop in front of a brownstone in Brooklyn.

"Where are we?"

"My place," she said. "I'm returning the favor and cooking you a meal."

He followed her inside and took her up on the offer of a shower while she cooked. He looked around her place as he walked through it to the guest room. He didn't want to assign too much significance to her bringing him here but a part of him felt like it meant a lot.

Willow had done a lot of soul searching the past week while Jack had been away and admitted to herself that revenge was no longer the only reason she wanted to spend time with Jack. She'd also been forced to acknowledge that for some reason Jack was important and that was it. Until she figured out what it was she had to learn from him she'd keep him close.

She glanced at the picture of her mama on the side of the fridge. It was her favorite picture of her mother, taken just minutes after Willow had been born. It was the happiest expression that Willow had ever seen on her mom's face.

She kept that picture where she could see it while she was cooking to remind herself of her mother's path. The one she didn't want to walk down. Her mother had been morbidly obese, and there were times when Willow had felt like drowning herself in food the way her mother had. She knew that it was the loneliness and doubt left behind when her father had abandoned them.

She heard the water of the shower stop and tried unsuccessfully not to imagine Jack naked. It wasn't too difficult to picture the rock-hard muscles that she'd felt when she'd hugged him, naked with water sliding down over his skin. She shuddered as a bolt of pure desire shot through her.

She reached for the eggs to crack them into the bowl so she could start making a frittata but really she was focused on a naked Jack in her guest room. She wanted him. That had always been a big part of why she'd liked him even back in high school.

She'd seldom met any other man who affected her the way he did. Even watching him on TV had turned her on. She used to pretend that the feelings coursing through her body were anger, but the truth was there was nothing wrong with her that a few hours in the sack couldn't cure.

"What's for breakfast?" Jack asked.

She turned around and saw he'd put on a pair of faded jeans, and a long-sleeved black T-shirt that fit him just right. His hair was still damp and tousled, stubble still covered his lower jaw and his feet were bare. He looked comfortable and sexy.

"Frittata," she said. "It's easier than an omelet for me. Is that okay?"

"Of course it is. My mom used to say beggars can't be choosers," he said, coming closer and leaning back against the countertop right next to her.

She could smell the fresh scent of her own soap on his skin and it smelled…delicious, she thought. She closed her eyes for a second and just breathed deeper.

"You okay?" he asked.

"Of course, when aren't I?"

"The other night…you sounded like you almost cared," he said. "I'm trying to be careful and not let it go to my head."

"I bet. You can't afford for your ego to get much bigger."

"Ah, there it is, the Willow I know," he said, and she could see the tiniest bit of disappointment in his eyes.

"I'm sorry. I don't like it when I'm forced to admit I care."

"Wow, that's honest. No one likes it because it leaves us vulnerable. But we all feel it."

"Do we?" she asked. "That ego is pretty big if you feel like you can speak for… Who are you speaking for? Just you and me or the entire world?"

He laughed. "God, woman, you definitely keep me humble."

She gave him a mock salute. "I try."

"Seriously, what changed?"

She concentrated on getting everything into the frying pan and ignored his question but Jack stood there like he had eternity and he'd happily wait forever for her answer.

"I…I need some closure with you," she said at last.

"You mentioned something I'd done in high school," he said.

"Yes," she said. All the ingredients were together

cooking. There was nothing for her to do but wait for it to set. She started cleaning up the kitchen.

Jack came up behind her and put his hands over hers, taking the dishes from her and placing them in the sink. He held her hands loosely in his as he turned her to face him. "Tell me. I'm sorry I don't remember anything bad happening between us. Just you helping me with English so I'd pass."

She took a deep breath. What was she going to say? How could she word this so that she didn't reveal too much? It was like he'd said a few moments ago—she didn't want to be vulnerable. Not to him.

"I have to watch the frittata or it will burn. Let's talk over breakfast, okay?" she asked.

He nodded. "I noticed the wine charms unopened on the counter. Didn't you like them?"

"Yes," she said. "But work has been keeping me pretty busy. Just haven't had time to use them yet, but I will on Monday."

"What happens on Monday?" he asked, crossing his arms over his chest.

"Girls' night," she said. The frittata had set so she shifted to the broiler to finish cooking.

"Nichole and Gail are your girls, right?"

"Yes. Do you remember them from high school?" she asked.

"No. We ran in different circles," he said. "Was that part of the problem between us?"

"Sort of. Let me set the table and we can eat."

"I'll help," he said. "What can I do?"

"Want to make the coffee?" she suggested, pointing to her Keurig machine and the mugs sitting next to it.

"Certainly."

Within a few minutes she had their food on the table

and was sitting right across from him but she didn't feel like eating and it didn't take a rocket scientist to realize that Jack didn't, either. He took a sip of his coffee and put his elbows on the table, leaning forward to take one of her hands.

"What'd I do back then?" he asked. "We can't move forward until we take care of that."

"Do you really want to move forward with me?" she asked.

"Do you have to keep asking?"

"Yes. I don't get it, Jack. No matter how I look at you and me we don't make sense."

"That's funny, because when I look at you, Willow, all I see is a woman I don't want to let go."

"Don't mess with me, Jack. I'm still not sure that you're not playing a game."

"I'm not," he said.

Jack had never been one to look away when Fate presented him with a second chance. And whatever he'd done to Willow in the past, he could fix, because he wanted her in his life now. He didn't know if it would be forever. To be honest he didn't believe in that sentiment. Everything ended and he knew that better than most people did. But he had also learned that he couldn't ignore experiences simply because they wouldn't last.

On this cold November Saturday morning he had been given an opportunity to spend time with Willow. He wanted to get this conversation out of the way so he could take her into his arms, carry her to her bedroom and make love to her in her own bed. Then he wanted to just lie in her arms under the covers and for this one day pretend the rest of the world didn't exist.

He didn't know if he'd get that chance but he was going to do everything in his power to make that happen. She'd cooked for him—something that only his mom had ever done. Sure, he'd dated other women and had some long-term relationships but the women he'd been involved with had never really done anything like this for him.

He felt cared for, and there was something so powerful in this moment that he was struggling to keep his hands to himself. He guessed that the way to his heart… or even lower…was through his stomach.

"Why are you smiling?" she asked. "There is something about you grinning that makes me nervous."

He had to shake his head because that comment was so Willow. Not the Willow he'd been texting with for the past few days but the Willow who'd refused every date he'd asked her on since May. "You make me happy. Even when you're prickly as a porcupine," he said.

"I'm not prickly," she said, reaching up and tucking a strand of her thick black hair behind her ear. He noticed she had small hoops in her ears this morning. He didn't think she'd ever worn earrings before. Then he noticed she had on makeup and unless he was mistaken, lipstick.

Had she dressed up for him?

"You look very pretty today," he said.

She blushed and shook her head. "Do you think by saying something nice I'll forget you just called me a porcupine? They aren't cute and cuddly."

"Well, you are," he said.

She shrugged. "Eat. You have to be starving," she said.

"Not for food. But I am hungry for you, Willow," he said, taking her hand and lifting it to his mouth. He brushed a kiss along the line of her knuckles.

She pulled her hand back. "I'm not…I can't do this." She stood.

"Why not?"

She shrugged again and turned her back on him. He felt as if he had her on the run and that was the last thing he wanted.

"Talk to me."

"I am. You're being difficult. You say I'm prickly but you're the one who is a pain."

"Why am I a pain?" he asked.

"Forget it," she said, sitting back down across from him and pushing the food around on her plate.

"What happened to that honesty you had earlier?" he asked. "I'm just a guy who is attracted to a girl who can be so stubborn."

She looked up at him with that dark chocolate gaze of hers and he felt a jolt go through his body. His blood started to run heavier. He thought he'd die if he didn't get her into bed soon.

Maybe that was the problem. They were talking when they should be doing. He was sitting here hesitating and letting her set the pace when that wasn't his way at all. Any other woman would have already been in his bed. But he'd waited because Willow could be…well, Willow.

"I don't try to be difficult," she said at last, licking her lips. He couldn't help but stare at her full mouth. He remembered the way she'd tasted when he'd kissed her just over a week ago. It couldn't have been as good as he remembered but a part of him knew it was.

"I just have to be in control," she said at last.

"I know. It's your defense mechanism. I hadn't realized it until this moment. You seem so tough that I never guessed there was anything you weren't confident about," he said at last. He stood up and walked around the table and drew her to her feet.

"What makes you think I'm not confident?" she asked.

"The way you're staring at me," he said. "You look like you're afraid of me. Why is that?"

With his hands on her hips, he held her still when she would have turned away. The curves of her body drove him mad. She was tall and slim, but so damned womanly. He wanted her out of the skintight jeans she wore and naked in his arms.

"I can't think when you are this close," she said.

He pulled her even closer but their bodies didn't touch except for his hands on her hips. Still, he could feel each exhalation of her breath against his neck.

"Why not?"

She lifted her hands to his shoulders. Then he felt her fingers along the back of his neck as she rose on her tiptoes and whispered in his ear, "I want you."

He shuddered as blood rushed to his groin and he hardened. "Good."

He lifted her off her feet and brought his mouth down on hers. He was tired of waiting for something that he knew he wanted. He needed her and the past week had only reinforced that fact.

He hoped that Willow never realized the power she had over him. Because if she did, he'd be on his knees.

Seven

Willow melted inside as Jack's mouth moved over hers, removing all her doubts at last. This was what she should have been focusing on since the beginning. Once she and Jack had sex, her obsession with him would fade and she'd be able to get back on track with her life.

She wrapped her legs around his hips and her arms around his shoulders. She tunneled her fingers through his hair and deepened the kiss. She kissed him with all the fear and longing and desire that had been plaguing her since she'd left his apartment little over a week ago.

He tasted of coffee and Jack. Something that was unique to him, and she realized that it was something she'd never get tired of tasting. His hands cupped her butt, his fingers moving over the tight denim that encased her and making her squirm in reaction. She loved the feel of his big hands on her.

He rubbed them up and down her back settling them

on her waist to hold her close against him as his tongue thrust deeper into her mouth. He kissed her like he was as addicted to her taste as she was to his.

She rocked her hips forward rubbing the center of her body against the tip of his erection. He moaned—the sound was earthy and sensual and she shivered again.

She felt like she was falling and then felt the solid wood of her butcher-block table underneath her. Jack leaned over her, caging her with his body. His breath sawed out of him and there was a slight flush to his skin. His pupils were dilated and his lips full and wet from her kisses.

He surrounded her, his hands on either side of her hips, his chest over her torso and his head right in front of hers. That sexy look in his blue, blue eyes made her shiver. She wanted this man.

"Enough playing around," he said. He found the sensitive spot beneath her ear and tongued it before nibbling his way down her neck until he encountered the collar of her sweater.

Jack was a dominant lover and though she usually liked to take charge, a part of her didn't want to with him. This was her break from reality and the more she wasn't herself the better she felt she'd be when they parted.

"Good," she agreed. "I was waiting for you to make the first move."

"That doesn't sound like the Willow I know. You go after what you want...don't you want me?"

He was right. Something about Jack had thrown her off her stride and made her forget that Willow Stead waited for no man. She put her hand on his chest and pushed him back until she stood up in front of him. Then she nudged him toward her chair, which she quickly pulled out from the table. He sat on it and she reached down to pull his black T-shirt up and off.

"That's better."

He rubbed his hand up his sternum and over the light dusting of hair there. He had just the right amount, she thought. And she'd been right about the rock-hard muscles there. She leaned down and ran her finger along the centerline of his body, following the tapering trail of hair.

She tweaked his flat brown nipples and watched as goose bumps spread across his body. He shifted in the chair, stretching his long legs out on either side of her. She moved a little closer, leaning over him, letting her hair fall gently over his chest. He shuddered and his hips jerked forward.

His pecs were heavy and well-defined and she lingered over them. Jack was hers for this moment in her tiny kitchen and she was going to enjoy every second of him. She straddled his lap and felt his hands on the hem of her sweater but she brushed them away.

"Not yet. I'm still exploring you."

"I want to do the same thing," he said. He pushed his hands up under her top and found the curve of her waist. He ran his fingers down her back over the seam of her jeans until he reached between her legs.

"I need to touch you, Willow," he said, her name a husky endearment on his lips. She shivered at the way he said it. But she wasn't going to let him take control now that she'd decided this was her show.

"It will distract me," she said. "And I want to know every inch of you by heart."

"There is time enough for that later. Right now I need to be inside you," he said. He drew her forward until her chest was pressed to his.

She shuddered as a pulse of pure sexual energy shot through her, pooling in her center. But she was in charge. She stepped back off his lap and smiled down at him.

"I'll decide when that happens." She narrowed her eyes and skimmed them over his body, watching his face for his reactions. She saw his pupils dilate and knew that he was turned on. "Show me how bad you want me."

"How will I prove it?" he asked, reaching out to rub his thumb over her lower lip. She nipped at it.

"Make me believe I'm the only woman in your life." She needed for Jack to work as hard at this thing between them as she was. She didn't want to be the only one out on a limb here. She knew there were really no words left to say between them right now. But she also knew that there was too much left unsaid.

"Do you doubt it?" he asked.

She did doubt it and yet at the same time no matter what she was afraid of she needed him here with her. She needed to know that he wanted her at least as much as she wanted him. And she wanted to be seduced.

He pushed to his feet. Jack moved his long lean athletic body with subtle grace. He took her hand and brought it to his mouth, sliding his lips along her knuckles and threading his fingers through hers. He placed her hand on his chest where she felt his heart beating like wild.

"My pulse is racing and I haven't done anything but look at you and imagine what you look like naked," he said.

She nodded, liking what she heard from him. "Tell me more."

It was hard to stay in control when he was so close and his body heat was wrapping around her. She wanted to push him back down in that chair and take him but he rubbed her hand over his chest and then let her go to reach for her sweater. This time he tugged it up and over her head before she could protest.

She felt his fingers on the point where her shoulder and neck met. With a light touch he stroked back and forth until her pulse grew a little bit heavier.

He leaned down and brushed his lips over that exact spot and then nibbled his way up to her ear as he pulled her closer to him. He whispered raw sexual words detailing what he intended to do to her and how hot the thought of it made him.

He caught her wrist in his hand and dragged it down his body to his erection. She loved the way his skin felt under the light dusting of hair. But his hardness felt even better to her touch. He was hard and long under the fabric of his jeans. She stroked him up and down.

He moaned her name, hips thrusting against her touch. She reached lower between his legs and rubbed him there. He shifted and moved closer to her.

"Touch me," he said, dragging her hands back up to his stomach and rubbing them against his sternum.

Sexual shivers spread over her as she leaned forward to nibble at his rock-hard stomach. She let her fingers continue to tease him through his denim jeans. She found his belly button and tongued it.

"Willow," he growled her name.

She smiled up at him, feeling very in control of herself and this sexy man. It was a powerful moment for her as a woman and she reveled in it. If she'd realized how much she'd been missing by keeping him at arm's length she would have said yes to him sooner.

She unbuttoned the fastening of his jeans and lowered his zipper, reaching past the cold metal to his hard-on where it pressed against the front of his cotton boxers.

She reached her finger inside the opening and touched the hot length. She maneuvered her other fingers in and wrapped them around him, stroking up and down.

Feeling a drop of moisture at the tip of his erection, she caught it on her finger and rubbed it into his skin. He shuddered and she felt another pulse of desire shoot through her.

He moaned her name and then captured her wrist and drew her hand out of his pants. She brought her hand from his grip and licked her finger where she could still taste the salty essence of him.

"Enough," he said. The gruff sexuality in his voice made her moist and ready for him. She wanted to climb onto his lap and take him. Force him deep inside of her so that she could claim every bit of him as her own.

He traced his fingers over her chest down to the globes of her smallish breasts where the push-up bra she wore made it look like she had cleavage. He lowered his head and she felt the brush of stubble from his jaw against her skin and then the warmth of his breath.

"So pretty," he said with a reverence that was at odds with the bluntness of his touch.

Then his tongue was right there tracing the line of fabric where her bra and skin met. It was the lightest of touches as his hands roamed up and down her back but it was exactly what she needed. She squirmed in his arms, found the opening of his jeans and reached inside to cup and stroke him.

He shimmied his hips and his jeans fell lower down to his thighs. She pushed them further down and he stepped out of them.

He undid her bra and once the fabric was loosened she shrugged her shoulders and let the bra fall down her arms and then dropped it to the floor. He lifted her in his arms again and set her up on the table. This time he stood back, staring down at her. She straightened her shoulders and let him look his fill.

She shivered at the passion in his eyes. He made her feel like she was the most entrancing woman in the world. He cupped both of her breasts, plumping them up and bringing them together. She glanced at him and was mesmerized by the look on his face.

He stared at her body with such awe and admiration. She swallowed hard against the emotions that threatened to overwhelm her. She never would have thought that she could elicit such feelings from Jack.

His fingers traced the circumference of each breast, making circles that slowly narrowed in until she felt the brush of his forefinger over her beaded nipples. He traced her areolas and she thrust her shoulders back to force her breasts into his touch. She caught her breath, afraid to breathe as he leaned down and laved first one and then the other with his tongue.

White-hot bolts of sensation shot through her as he continued to lick at her nipple while he stroked her other one with his hand. She was caught in a delicate trap with his fingers and tongue holding her prisoner. She reached for him, grabbing his hips and drawing him closer until she felt him nudging at her center through the fabric of her jeans.

She wanted him naked. She was tired of playing sexual games. She freely admitted to herself that she'd only done it to see how far she could push him. And because she'd wanted to prove to herself that she was still the boss.

But the more he touched her the less in control she felt. She knew that she had absolutely no willpower where he was concerned. And for once that didn't really matter.

She needed to be pressed against his hot erection and feel him inside her. She pushed his underwear off his hips and he stepped out of them.

He undid her jeans and she lifted herself up so he could pull them down her legs and toss them on the floor with her tiny thong panties. Then he leaned over her, letting his furry chest brush over her sensitized nipples. She shivered with desire and he leaned in closer to whisper in her ear.

"Do you like that?"

"Yes," she whispered back in a soft tone that was husky to her own ears.

"Good. Do you know I want you?"

"Yes," she said.

"If you can still talk then I'm not doing a good enough job," he said, pushing her knees farther apart.

"Lean back," he ordered.

She grabbed his hips and pulled him forward to her until she felt the tip of his erection touching her. She sighed and opened her legs wider to accommodate his hips. He thrust against her so that the length of him rubbed over her most sensitive flesh.

She was wet and ready for him but still he hesitated. He leaned down and found her mouth with his. His tongue thrusted into her the way she longed for other parts of him to, but still he kept her on the edge.

She drew her hands up and down his back finding those pronounced hip bones of his and holding on to him while she wrapped her legs high around his waist. She urged her body forward on his next thrust and felt the tip of him just inside the entrance of her body.

She sighed as he pulled back, bracing both hands on the table next to her head.

"Are you on the pill?"

She didn't understand the words at first, frustrated that he'd teased her with so little of what she wanted and then pulled out.

"What?"

"The pill?"

"Yes," she said.

He nodded and lowered his mouth to hers again. His tongue swept over hers as his hands danced down her body, reigniting embers that were still glowing white-hot.

His hands lingered over her breasts, cupping them. He rubbed his palms in circles over her nipples until she arched her back and felt as if he didn't enter her at that moment she was going to die.

She grabbed the back of his head and thrust her tongue into his mouth. She lifted her hips and grabbed the back of his thigh with her other hand drawing him closer.

He pulled his mouth from hers and all she could do was stare up at him. He put his hands on her thighs and opened her legs even farther and she watched as he caressed her with one hand. He parted her nether lips and then she felt the brush of his finger over the sensitive bud there.

He made circles over her flesh and then tapped it in a rhythm that made everything inside of her clench. She arched her hips as a climax washed over her. He kept touching her between her legs until the sensations started to subside and then she felt him back at her entrance. He nudged his way into her body one slow inch at a time and thrust gently back and forth.

"That's all you're getting until you come again," he said.

Sensation feathered up her spine and she knew he wouldn't have to wait long. She pulled his head down to hers and whispered darkly sexual words in his ear and she felt his hips jerk.

Suddenly he was driving himself as deep as he could inside her and she felt the first burst of sensation as her climax ripped through her. This one so much more satisfying because Jack was there with her. He kept thrusting into her and then she felt his hips jerk, a flood of warmth jetting into her.

She was shaking and he was sweating as he leaned down over her. His chest resting on her breasts, his head nestled into the curve of her neck. He dropped the softest, sweetest kisses on her shoulder and it was all she could do not to turn and drop a kiss on the top of his head.

She wrapped her arms around him and her legs around his waist and held him to her. She was careful not to let herself get too attached to this moment but she couldn't help it. This was Jack Crown, the man she'd never thought she'd have in her bed.

And she had to say that her dreams were nothing compared to the reality of having him. He stood up and pulled out of her body. Suddenly she felt vulnerable and shy and she sat up, pushing her long hair back behind her shoulder.

"Um…I need to clean up," he said.

As far as postcoital endearments went, those sucked, she thought. She'd slept with other guys who'd left her as soon as the deed was done but she'd expected something more from Jack. She'd forgotten that by his own definition he was still a frog. Hoping that her kiss would

YOUR READER'S SURVEY "THANK YOU" FREE GIFTS INCLUDE:

- 2 Harlequin® Desire® books
- 2 lovely surprise gifts

▶ DETACH AND MAIL CARD TODAY! ▶

PLEASE FILL IN THE CIRCLES COMPLETELY TO RESPOND

1) What type of fiction books do you enjoy reading? (Check all that apply)
❍ Suspense/Thrillers ❍ Action/Adventure ❍ Modern-day Romances
❍ Historical Romance ❍ Humour ❍ Paranormal Romance

2) What attracted you most to the last fiction book you purchased on impulse?
❍ The Title ❍ The Cover ❍ The Author ❍ The Story

3) What is usually the greatest influencer when you plan to buy a book?
❍ Advertising ❍ Referral ❍ Book Review

4) How often do you access the internet?
❍ Daily ❍ Weekly ❍ Monthly ❍ Rarely or never.

5) How many NEW paperback fiction novels have you purchased in the past 3 months?
❍ 0 - 2 ❍ 3 - 6 ❍ 7 or more

YES! I have completed the Reader's Survey. Please send me the 2 FREE books and 2 FREE gifts (gifts are worth about $10) for which I qualify. I understand that I am under no obligation to purchase any books, as explained on the back of this card.

225/326 HDL FNPU

FIRST NAME LAST NAME

ADDRESS

APT.# CITY

STATE/PROV. ZIP/POSTAL CODE

Offer limited to one per household and not applicable to series that subscriber is currently receiving.
Your Privacy – The Reader Service is committed to protecting your privacy. Our Privacy Policy is available online at www.ReaderService.com or upon request from the Reader Service. We make a portion of our mailing list available to reputable third parties that offer products we believe may interest you. If you prefer that we not exchange your name with third parties, or if you wish to clarify or modify your communication preferences, please visit us at www.ReaderService.com/consumerschoice or write to us at Reader Service Preference Service, P.O. Box 9062, Buffalo, NY 14269. Include your complete name and address.

© 2012 HARLEQUIN ENTERPRISES LIMITED
® and ™ are trademarks owned and used by the trademark owner and/or its licensee. Printed in the U.S.A.

HD-SUR-11/12

The Reader Service — Here's How It Works:

Accepting your 2 free books and 2 free gifts (gifts valued at approximately $10.00) places you under no obligation to buy anything. You may keep the books and gifts and return the shipping statement marked "cancel." If you do not cancel, about a month later we'll send you 6 additional books and bill you just $4.30 each in the U.S. or $4.49 each in Canada. That is a savings of at least 14% off the cover price. It's quite a bargain! Shipping and handling is just 50¢ per book in the U.S. and 75¢ per book in Canada.* You may cancel at any time, but if you choose to continue, every month we'll send you 6 more books, which you may either purchase at the discount price or return to us and cancel your subscription.

*Terms and prices subject to change without notice. Prices do not include applicable taxes. Sales tax applicable in N.Y. Canadian residents will be charged applicable taxes. Offer not valid in Quebec. Books received may not be as shown. All orders subject to credit approval. Credit or debit balances in a customer's account(s) may be offset by any other outstanding balance owed by or to the customer. Please allow 4 to 6 weeks for delivery. Offer available while quantities last.

If offer card is missing write to: The Reader Service, P.O. Box 1867, Buffalo, NY 14240-1867 or visit: www.ReaderService.com

NO POSTAGE
NECESSARY
IF MAILED
IN THE
UNITED STATES

BUSINESS REPLY MAIL
FIRST-CLASS MAIL PERMIT NO. 717 BUFFALO, NY
POSTAGE WILL BE PAID BY ADDRESSEE

THE READER SERVICE
PO BOX 1341
BUFFALO NY 14240-8571

turn him into a prince. "That's it? That's all you're going to say? My kisses obviously weren't special enough to turn you from a frog."

"Dammit, I'm not sure what else to say," he admitted. "I want to take you in my arms and carry you down the hall to the bedroom and then spend the rest of the day making love to you."

"Then why don't you?" she asked because there were times when she wanted to pretend she lived in this fantasy world with Jack. A world where he thought she was hot and sexy and neither of them had a past or a future to worry about.

"I'm not sure you're ready for it," he said. "And I'm not sure I am, either."

She nodded. "Go clean up."

Aching deep inside, she hopped off the table. She wrapped her arms around her waist, but it wasn't enough of a comfort. She felt raw and exposed and all the good feelings she'd had just seconds earlier were gone.

Then she felt Jack's big hand on her shoulder and the other one at her waist. "Damn it."

"What?"

"I can't do this. I know it would be better to give you some time to adjust to things, but I need you, Willow. And for once I'm taking what I want."

He lifted her in his arms and carried her down the hall to her bedroom. They spent the rest of the day in her full-size bed—which was too small for Jack—making love and pretending that the real world didn't exist.

"Thank you for this," he said as the afternoon started to darken into evening. "I think we had a date planned for tonight. How about I head home and you get dolled up?"

She nodded, afraid to say anything. Her emotions

were too close to the surface and if she wasn't careful she was going to reveal too much.

She put on her robe and got out of bed when all she really wanted to do was to stay there curled in his arms. God, not knowing if he'd died in that shark attack had shaken her too much. What had she been thinking to bring him here? If she thought she'd had a hard time keeping him out of her mind when he'd been just a boy from her past how was she going to do it now that he'd slept in her bed.

She let him leave, then stood in front of the mirror staring at her tousled hair and the red marks on her neck from his kisses and beard stubble and wondered where her willpower had gone.

Eight

Jack tried to keep his mind on the date night he'd promised Willow but really he was just glad he'd gotten out of her bed when he did. His temptation had been to stay there and wrap himself around her. To hold on to her so she'd never disappear from his life. And he knew that when he felt that way about anything it was doomed to end.

He entered his apartment and showered, washing the smell of sex and Willow off his body. He'd checked his email and voice mail earlier to try to get back into the real world but his mind still lingered in that small bed in Brooklyn where he'd held Willow.

He got dressed and made a reservation at one of the most exclusive restaurants in town. One of the many perks to his lifestyle was the fact that he could get a table anywhere when he needed one. And like his little hissy fit about the exotic fruit basket, he tried to keep those instances to a minimum but at times it was very convenient.

Then he tried to forced himself to get back into work mode. Sleeping with Willow hadn't eased the ache in his soul. He didn't suddenly know her any better; in fact, she was more of a mystery now than she had been before. He wondered if he hadn't screwed himself by getting involved with her.

Willow had him tied in knots. No matter what he did he felt like he still couldn't figure her out. What was it about her that made her so different from other women?

Everything.

Everything, from her tough-as-nails exterior to that gooey soft inner woman that she was desperate to keep hidden from the world, pushed his buttons. Why?

His phone pinged and he glanced down to see a text message from Rhia Montaine. PJ was coming out of his coma. She didn't have a good cell phone signal in the hospital but would welcome a call from Jack on the hospital phone.

He took a deep breath, as the text was just the reminder he needed to rein things in with Willow. Earlier he'd been desperate to hold on to her but this forced him to remember the reality of his life.

Nothing lasted. Not even the good times. Everything ended, no matter what he did to protect it.

He dialed the hospital and waited a few minutes for the call to be connected. With cell phones it was odd to have to use a traditional operator to get in touch with someone. He had a flashback to high school when that was the only way he'd been able to communicate with his single mom when she was at work.

"Hello," Rhia answered, sounding tired and a little bit stressed-out. He wondered how many calls she'd had to deal with today. The production company had hired a bodyguard to keep the paparazzi away from the hospital room. Though PJ was well known in the surfing world, Rhia was an internationally famous actress and the cameras followed her wherever she went.

"It's Jack. How's our guy?" Jack asked, keeping his voice gentle, trying to be soothing when he was anything but calm inside.

"Awake, but he's still weak," Rhia said.

It was good to hear that PJ had come out of the coma. He was afraid to ask anything else, though. Did PJ blame Jack for the lost leg?

"How are you?" he asked instead.

"Exhausted, but also very happy. Oh, Jack, I am so relieved that he's awake and cracking wise. He asked if you were okay."

"Of course I am. Why wouldn't I be?" Jack asked.

"You were shaken, too," Rhia said. "I saw you before you got on that plane, remember?"

"Well, I'm good. Can I talk to him?"

"Let me check."

He heard Rhia's muted voice but not her words as she talked to PJ and a moment later there was some rustling on the other end of the phone and then a very weak and gruff voice said, "I hope that was exciting enough for your TV viewers."

Jack shook his head and laughed, as he knew PJ was hoping he would, but his heart ached at his physically virile friend sounding so damned weak. "Showboater. Always trying to outdo everyone else."

"Gotta keep my rep as a badass," PJ said, but he didn't sound tough.

"You've earned it now."

There was a prolonged silence leaving Jack to wonder

if PJ had fallen asleep. That was probably a blessing—it would let Jack end one of the hardest conversations he'd ever had. Usually he was the one in a hospital bed. Usually? He guessed he was getting melodramatic. One time he'd been the guy in the hospital bed and it was so much easier than being this guy. The one who escaped the incident scott-free.

He finally understood why Wayne McKenzie, the tackle who'd brought him down, called him once a year. The other guy had guilt. Until this moment Jack had thought it was because of the injury that he'd sustained but now he knew it was because life for Wayne had gone on and for Jack it was changed forever.

He heard a very soft sound as PJ cleared his throat.

"Thank you. If you hadn't acted so quickly, I'd be dead."

"You're welcome," Jack said. PJ would never know how glad he was that he'd been there to help him. And if Jack was completely honest he was glad that he hadn't been the one to take that first wave. "I don't have enough friends to let one go easily."

PJ laughed, and it was a genuine sound that made Jack feel a little better about his friend's chances of recovering. "That's because you think you're all that."

"I do," Jack admitted. He realized that PJ and Willow would get along very well because both of them thought nothing of taking shots at his ego. That bit of insight made him realize that Willow was indeed different from other women in his life. She might be the first real person he'd been involved with for a long, long time.

"Doc's coming in to look at his handiwork. I lost the leg," PJ said.

"Ah, man. I'm sorry," Jack said, even though he'd known the leg was gone before he'd left L.A. The injuries had been too massive to save it and he'd sat in a tense waiting room with Rhia while the surgery had been performed.

"It's cool. I'm already trying to figure out how I'll be able to surf one-legged. Maybe I'll invent something new that will set the world on fire."

"I'm sure you will," Jack said. PJ wasn't the kind of man to be kept down by anything.

"Later, man."

"Later," Jack said as he hung up the phone.

PJ's attitude was good but Jack remembered his own operation and waking up with a scarred leg. His injuries hadn't been as severe as PJ's of course, but those first few days he'd just been happy to be alive. Then as time went on and he physically recovered he realized that he'd never be able to play again. He made a note to check in with PJ again soon because he had a feeling once his friend left the hospital things were going to get a little too real. And Jack had been there.

He stood up as he got ready to head to the restaurant. He had been there and he always survived. Whatever happened with Willow he'd come out on the other side and move on. He wished he could feel differently or believe that maybe they could have forever, but that wasn't the kind of guy he was. He never had been.

Which reminded him that he'd done something to her in the past that she hadn't been able to forgive. He needed to find out what that was. Maybe he was back in Willow's life to help her with something before he moved on.

He tried to tell himself that his attitude toward life and Fate was healthy but a part of him ached at the thought of not keeping Willow as his own for the rest of his life.

He shook that off as he left his apartment and headed to the restaurant where he was meeting Willow. Live for the moment was his mantra until he saw her walking toward him. Then he wanted to change his life and his beliefs because he wanted to keep her.

Willow was glad that Jack had left when he had because it gave her a chance to get back to normal. *Yeah, right.* She'd left normal the moment she'd gone to the airport to pick him up.

She didn't know what she was going to do. Her plan for revenge was out the window because at this point she couldn't be cold and walk away from him. She didn't know if she ever had been able to do that. She wondered if she'd used anger as a protective buffer to keep him at arm's length until now.

Unable to figure out what else to do she picked up the phone and called Nichole.

"Yo dog, what up?" Nichole said.

"Huh? Why are you talking like a wannabe white rapper?" she asked.

"I'm giving my husband a hard time. He's ignoring me to do business," Nichole said. "What's up?"

"Conner's right there?"

"Yes, but he's on a conference call. He's been on the phone for the last twenty minutes…okay, I'm in the kitchen out of earshot. What's going on?"

Willow took a deep breath. She had never really been one to talk about her own life. She was the best listener of anyone in their little threesome but she always kept her own confidence. "I slept with Jack."

"Yay! About time," Nichole said. "Right? It was a good thing?"

"I don't know. I mean, yes, it was good. But I don't think it was a smart move for me."

"Hold on. Let me conference Gail in. I'm on Jack's side since I think he's perfect for you."

"What? How can someone who's traveling all the time be perfect for me?" Willow asked.

"I'll tell you in a second. Gail needs to be in on this. Don't tell her I said this but she's smart about people."

Willow agreed with Nichole and held the line for a minute until Gail came on. "So you slept with Jack."

"Yes. What should I do now?" Willow asked. "For once I don't know what the next step should be. I mean if I were still going for revenge I guess I could go to dinner and then dump him."

"Are you still thinking about walking away from him so he knows what that feels like?" Gail asked.

"No," Willow said. She knew she couldn't do that now that she'd gotten to know Jack. "He wouldn't be the only one to get hurt if I did that."

"Is it that serious?" Nichole asked.

"I just don't know. Sleeping with him…well, I thought I could make it just sex but somehow when he left here this afternoon I knew it wasn't. I guess I sort of knew it before when he sent me that damned frog prince."

"What frog prince?" Nichole asked.

"He sent me these little gifts when he was in L.A. One of them was a trinket box shaped like a frog prince…."

"I didn't know he sent you a gift."

"Well, he did," Willow said. "And that confused everything."

"Okay, so what do we need to figure out?" Gail asked.

"If I should walk away now before I get in any deeper. I think I could and not get hurt," Willow said.

"Oh, honey," Nichole said. "I don't think you can. He sent you gifts, he's been texting you and—"

"Let's not put too much emphasis on that. He's wooing you like any guy would do. You have to be smart about this," Gail said. "Let's put Willow first. What is going to be best for you?"

"Like Nic said, he's wooing me and no guy has done that before. I like it."

"Okay. So did he ask you out again?" Gail asked.

"Yes. We have a dinner date tonight. He left to get ready for it. He's sending a car for me in an hour. Should I go?"

"Yes," Nichole said.

"I think you have to," Gail said. "You want to. I hear it in your voice. Why are you hesitating?"

Willow didn't want to talk about the past with Jack and she knew that was the crux of the matter. "If we'd never met before he came on the show I'd be there in a heartbeat."

"Then pretend you didn't," Nichole said.

"I can't. He doesn't remember standing me up on prom night," she said. "What does that say about him? And me, that I slept with him when he can't remember the one thing that shaped me and my attitude toward men."

"It says he moves on and leaves the past behind him. It also says you want him enough to risk being hurt again," Gail said.

"No. I'm in control this time," Willow said, but the words sounded hollow even to her.

"Right, I thought I could be Conner's mistress and not fall for him," Nichole said.

"And I thought I could fix Russell without letting him into my heart," Gail said.

"Why? We are all smart women," Willow said.

"Because men make women stupid," Nichole said.

"No, the right man can make one woman stupid," Gail said. "It's specific to one guy and one girl."

"Jack's my guy," Willow said.

"Probably because of the past he's tied in your head to love. I can't say what you're feeling now," Gail said. "But we're your friends and we're never going to judge you. If you want him..."

"Then go and get him," Nichole said. "And I'm not just saying that to win the spa day."

Willow tried to laugh but she was so confused. She didn't feel stupid because of Jack, she felt unsure. And a lack of confidence was the one thing she hated most in the world.

"Thanks, ladies."

"No problem. We always have your back," Gail said.

"And you've always had ours," Nichole added.

Willow hung up the phone, still feeling no closer to deciding if she should go or not. But something that Gail had said kept circling around in her mind. What does Willow want?

She thought about calling Jack with some lame excuse and sitting at home all night, but then realized she'd been hiding away long enough.

She got dressed in a slinky number she'd bought with Kat at a designer sale last week. Standing there staring at herself in the mirror, she thought she hardly resembled the girl she'd been in Texas. Yet at the same time she didn't look like her more recent self, either. Jack had forced her to change—not intentionally, but all the same the change was there. She saw it in her own eyes.

She wondered if Nic had thought that this would be the outcome of her going to drinks with Jack. Her friend had thought she needed to change, but Willow was afraid of it.

Her phone rang and she answered it.

"This is Home James Cars. Your driver is waiting for you at the curb."

The drive from Brooklyn to the city, despite being a long one thanks to traffic, didn't bring any resolution to her thoughts. When she finally arrived at her destination, she tipped her driver and entered the restaurant.

She spotted Jack waiting for her at the bar. He wore a dinner jacket and a tie and his hair was slicked down. He stood up and approached when he saw her. She shivered as she remembered that naked muscled body of his and knew that she was doomed. She was never going to be rational about a man who made her feel what Jack did.

Jack realized immediately that Willow felt as out of place as he did. It was as if they'd gotten too close and now there was no way to go back to the safe place they'd been before. The conversation was awkward with stops and starts and he realized that he was partially to blame because he was afraid to let her see how much she affected him.

He'd spent his entire life half hoping that things would last and then being resigned when they didn't. His mom would have said that was a self-fulfilling prophecy and he guessed he'd have to admit that she was right again.

Finally over dessert, when he'd learned that she didn't care for sparkly vampires and thought that too many people in Hollywood didn't get the viewing public, he put his elbows on the table and leaned toward her.

"Why did you pick me up today?" he asked. "You didn't have to and that move was a game changer."

She tucked a strand of hair behind her ear and then

seemed to remember that she'd left the piece hanging to frame her face in the updo and untucked it. "I…I don't know."

She took a sip of her wine and looked away from him at the other diners and then back at him. "When I wasn't sure if you were dead or alive…it changed something inside of me. I stopped thinking about revenge—"

"Why do you want revenge? What did I do?"

She took a big swallow of her wine and then set the glass down. "Do you remember me in high school?"

"Yes. You were my tutor for English. We met in the early mornings before football practice."

"That's right. What else do you remember?" she asked.

He knew he was missing something but what? "We used to talk. I remember you were determined to win a Pulitzer and get out of Frisco. You used to say that you craved big cities and big minds that didn't judge."

She leaned back and gave him a shrewd look. "I'd forgotten how arrogant I was. I thought I was better than everyone else in our class."

"It didn't come off that way," he said. "You just seemed like someone who knew what she wanted from life. Me, I just wanted to win State and get that big shiny ring for myself. But you were already looking beyond high school."

She bit her lower lip. "I was. Um…you asked me to prom and stood me up."

"What?"

"Sorry I had to blurt that out but there was no other way. I don't want to remember that girl I was. We had been in a session and you brought up prom and asked me if I was going… I said no, you said, well, if you want to go I'll take you."

Suddenly he remembered. He'd wanted to do something nice for Willow, who still had two more years in the town she'd wanted desperately to get out of. He'd thrown the winning touchdown the previous fall to make his team state champs and that dewy April morning it had seemed right to make the offer.

"I don't remember standing you up," he said, wiping his mouth and looking away from her. "Is that what you thought?"

It wasn't what she thought—it was what had happened. She'd been dressed up, even had her hair done, and he'd never shown up. She shook her head, tossing her napkin down on the table and standing up. "It doesn't matter. I'm going to the ladies' room."

He watched her walk away, trying to remember more of that time. Until she'd mentioned prom, he'd forgotten all about it. Though many of his classmates had predicted that high school would be the high point of his life, it hadn't been. It had just been one more leg of a journey that had taken him off in another direction.

But it had shaped Willow. He remembered going to her house… Oh, no. Now he remembered what had happened. He'd stopped by two days before prom to check and make sure he had the time right to pick her up. And Mrs. Stead had confronted him.

She'd known who he was since he'd received a lot of local press coverage after winning the State Championship and getting a full-ride scholarship to the University of Texas. She'd told him in no uncertain terms that her daughter wasn't to be toyed with. He'd been a high school senior and not willing to commit to anything other than prom. Which is when Mrs. Stead had told him that it would be a kindness to leave Willow alone since her daughter loved him.

He saw Willow coming back to the table and remembered with shame how he'd acted back then. He'd assumed her mom would have said something to her about him not coming, but now he guessed she hadn't. And he'd been too embarrassed to say anything to her about that day.

"I'm sorry," he said.

She shook her head. "I…I thought you were a different guy back then. I know you were immature."

"I was. I can't even relate to that kid anymore. But that's no excuse. I'm so sorry, Willow."

From the look in her eyes, he knew he wasn't going to gain absolution from her with just a few words. He didn't think he deserved it, either. Why would he have just walked away without saying anything? he asked himself. He knew why. Back then he was the biggest thing in Frisco and he had thought Mrs. Stead had crossed a line.

"I was an ass," he said. "I'm not that guy anymore."

She almost smiled and he knew that she wanted to forgive him. "What happened? Why didn't you show up?" she asked.

"Your mom warned me off. She said that you were…" He paused, realizing how embarrassing this might be for her.

"What did she say? When did you talk to my mom?" she asked.

"I stopped by after school two days before prom and you weren't there. Your mom knew who I was and told me that I shouldn't mess around with you because you had feelings for me."

She turned red, and he realized his explanation wasn't doing him any good.

"She just said if I wasn't serious about you it would be better if I didn't take you to prom. And I… Well, it ticked me off. I was a star at school. Any other girl's parents would have been excited if I'd asked their daughter out."

"So you got mad and decided to stand me up," she said.

"I just figured your mom would say something to you when I didn't show up," he said. "And I think I already admitted I was an ass. I wish I'd been more mature back then."

"Me, too," she said. "But you have to understand that I spent a lot of time resenting you."

"Resentment? Was that it?"

"No, I hated you. I wished bad things would happen to you, but no matter what happened you always sort of rolled with it and came out on the other side with an even better life."

"Let me take care of the check so we can get out of here and talk. My life isn't the bed of roses you think it is."

He paid the bill and they walked outside where a light snow had started to fall. "Do you mind taking a walk? I don't want to be cooped up in the car."

She wore a heavy wool coat and had a scarf around her neck so he knew she'd be warm enough.

"Where will we walk?"

"Want to take a look at the shop windows on Fifth?" he suggested.

It seemed like something a normal couple would do on a date and he didn't want to admit how relieved he was when she agreed.

Nine

The cool breeze on her cheeks made it impossible to dwell in the past. The contrition she sensed in Jack just reaffirmed what she was coming to know of him. He was so much more than the boy she remembered from so long ago. She was glad to be here with him right now.

She reached out and took his hand. He glanced over at her in surprise and intertwined his fingers with hers.

"Nothing with you ever goes the way I think it will," he said.

"Good. I don't like to be predictable," she said. "I'm beginning to believe you don't, either."

"Of course I don't," he said, pulling her out of the foot traffic and into a little alcove that was tucked into the side of a building. "Every time I get comfortable something happens to shake me up."

"What do you mean?"

"Just that what you see as me always landing on my

feet is my having to figure out once again how to start over," he said.

She tipped her head to the side to study him. Some snow had fallen on his hair and it was tousled and wet but he still looked sexy and confident. He didn't seem to her like a man who'd started over from scratch.

"All of those experiences have made you the man you are today," she said. "You are so strong and capable. Now that I think about it, I probably shouldn't have worried about you in that shark attack. I should have known that you'd come out of that safe."

He shook his head. "Yeah, I always survive but there are scars, Willow."

"I know," she said, reaching up to give him a one-armed hug. "I'm sorry I'm being lighthearted after the toll those events have had on you."

"Do you see it?" he asked.

"I don't think so. You've given me something to think about, but I can't let go of the past as easily as you do."

"Fair enough," he said. "I'll keep apologizing even though I know my words can't heal the past."

Yet a part of her felt as if he could with that attitude. He had been wrong to just now show up, and she knew him well enough to know it had been his bruised ego that had caused his actions. She couldn't forgive him easily, but she had a suspicion that eventually she would do so. She liked him. Dammit, what was wrong with her? Why did Jack affect her heart this way?

"See, we are finding our way to each other," she said. And for a moment she felt a ray of hope. Like maybe this time she and Jack were on the right track. But to what? She'd never imagined herself married and just because her friends were all happily settled into monogamous relationships didn't mean she craved one, too. Besides this was Jack she was thinking about.

"Yes, we are. This part of the journey is turning into a very interesting one," he said.

"This part? Do you still think we'll end up diverging at some point?"

"I can't see how we won't. There isn't one person in my life who's always stayed with me."

"Your mom," she said, stepping back from him.

They started walking again. The windows seemed magical all decorated for fall. Some eager merchants had already put up holiday scenes and she realized that she didn't feel confident that she and Jack would still be together then. Maybe this thing between them was just sex. Sex and closure from the past for her.

"My mom died before I graduated college," he said. "I'm not whining. She gave me everything and I tried to make her life a little easier before she died."

"That's true," she said. Because what else could she say? She just imagined Jack with a big extended family and lots of friends. She knew she pictured him that way because it was the opposite of what she had. Her mom had been an only child and when she'd died, Willow had been alone.

Totally alone except for Gail and Nichole, who were her soul sisters. She didn't know how she would have survived without those two.

"Surely you have some good friends from high school and college," she said.

"I know some people from back then, but they don't get in touch too often except to ask me to donate time or call someone famous and ask them to do a charity gig. Do you ever have that?"

"No," Willow said. "I didn't keep in touch with anyone from back home except for Gail and Nichole. Since my mom's gone I don't go back. I don't really miss Texas much. This is my home now."

"I miss it sometimes," he said. "But I don't get back. I mean, what's the point of going back? I'm living a different life now. And so are you. It's funny to me that you were so fixated on the past when you really don't want to be back there."

She realized that he was giving her a little too much credit. She'd kept a list of anyone who ever did her wrong. It was just the way she'd always been. She'd felt like she had a chip on her shoulder. "I wasn't fixated on the past, Jack. I wanted revenge."

"Why? Given the girl you were I can't imagine prom meant that much to you," he said.

There was a lot of truth to what he said but there was also the universal realism that every girl wanted to have a handsome boy ask her to prom. It didn't matter what she told her friends. Willow had wanted to have that fairy-tale dream come true on prom night. "I really liked you and you hurt me. I wanted to hurt you like that," she said.

"Bloodthirsty, aren't you?" he asked.

"Yes, I am. I know you survive by moving on. I did it by planning ways to get back at others."

"I wasn't the only one?" he asked.

"Well, you are the only one from Texas. I try not to make the same mistakes over and over. But there was a producer who screwed me over when I first got into the business."

"What happened?"

"I got more successful than him. He asked me for a job last year and I turned him down."

"Willow."

"I know, it wasn't nice but he was a total jerk and fired me so he could hire his girlfriend. I had to live with Gail for six months."

"I'm sorry. Did you feel better after you did that?" he asked.

"No. I felt bad. I mean, the economy is horrible now, and if he hadn't fired me I wouldn't have started my own company, so he sort of did me a favor."

He shook his head. "What did you do?"

"I called a friend and they made him an offer. He doesn't know I had anything to do with it."

She shouldn't have shared that, she thought afterward but she wanted Jack to know that even though she wanted to feel better about the people who'd hurt her in the past she'd never been able to really hurt someone the way she'd been hurt. She didn't want anyone to ever feel as bad as she had. And as he linked their hands together and continued walking she realized that was especially true about him.

Jack had learned more than he'd expected from Willow on this dinner date and as he stood next to her holding her hand, he wondered if he'd made a huge mistake. But she was looking up at him like he was something special and he felt bigger than he had before. He felt like for once he was the good guy in the tale and not the sidekick.

His entire life he'd felt like the sidekick because he wasn't assured of a happy ending. Was this his chance? It wasn't going to happen tonight, he knew that.

"Want to come back to my place?" he asked. "You never did get to see my bedroom."

"I...I'm not really sure. I want to say yes but I feel

too raw right now. You've made me face things about myself I usually just ignore."

"Sorry," he said, but he wasn't. She made him feel so vulnerable that it was only fair he did the same to her. Ms. In Control finally wasn't and he couldn't help but feel a little pleased with that.

"No, you're not. You like it because now you have something to hold over me," she said.

He shook his head as he led her into a small coffee shop and took a back-corner booth so they could have some privacy. She sat down on the vinyl-covered banquette first and instead of sitting across from her, he slid in beside her and put his arm around her shoulder.

"You're crowding me."

"Good. I want to crowd you and force you out of your comfort zone because every second since I walked onto the set of *Sexy & Single* that's what you've done to me. You think I'm trying to one-up you when really all I'm trying to do is find a way to keep the scales balanced."

She swallowed and he watched the way she shrunk back into herself. He knew he was hitting her too hard tonight but seeing how close PJ had come to dying, knowing that his own track record meant that he might not get everything he wanted with Willow—well, he just couldn't afford to wait around for her to start caring about him. He needed her to do that now.

"Why are you acting like this?"

"PJ almost died. He just got married, Willow. He just started a life with the one person he wants to share it with and it was almost wiped out. Do you know how many times I've had to start over alone?"

"At least once."

"Four times," he said.

"Okay. What does that have to do with me?" she

asked. “I’m doing my best to treat you like I would any other guy I’m dating.”

“I don’t want that. I want you to treat me like…well, like me. So that I’m not one of many who could fit in your life but the only one who can.”

“We’ve only been dating for a little more than a week,” she said.

He understood what she was saying. In his rational mind he knew she was right but for him this was more intense. For him life had a way of boiling down to months instead of years and he wanted every second to count with Willow.

“Whatever,” he said, sliding out of the booth and then sitting down across from her on the other side of the table. “My bad. Let’s order some coffee and then I’ll call the car to take you home. We have an early day tomorrow, right?”

“Yes, and the next day. Tomorrow we’re at Pablo’s East for a wine tasting and then the next day Peter and Deidre are doing a Toys for Tots charity thing.”

“I don’t want to talk about work,” he said.

“Well, I’m in charge now, so we have to get these details out of the way. Unless you want to talk about the future.”

“Hell,” he said. “There’s no give in you, is there, Willow? It’s either work or me saying something I might regret, and I don’t want to do that.”

She nodded. “Okay. Well, we’re doing the Toys for Tots thing at the family-owned Box of Toys in the Hamptons. My friends…Nichole and Conner invited me to join them for dinner when the shoot is over. Would you like to come with me?”

Why should he? She was going to keep manipulating him—then he realized she wasn’t trying to do anything to him. She was trying to protect herself and he really couldn't blame her for that since he was trying to do the exact same thing. Maybe the dinner invitation was an olive branch.

"I'd love to. How are you getting down there?" he asked.

"Helicopter with Deidre and Peter. You are, too. Didn't you read the email I sent you?" she asked.

"I haven't exactly had time today. I was kidnapped by a sexy woman," he said.

She ignored that. "I didn't kidnap you. You know I talked to Deidre before the last date and realized that no matter how wise she seems when giving advice to others, she's the same as you and I when it comes to being confused in her own life."

"What made you realize that?" he asked. He signaled the waiter to bring them two coffees.

"She was afraid to have her heart broken," Willow said, leaning forward and looking him square in the eye. "Just like me. I'm not stringing you along."

"Yeah, I know that now. I'm a guy, though, and sometimes I just lose my temper."

"I don't see what being a guy has to do with that. I lose my temper all the time," she said with that grin of hers that made him want to kidnap her and keep her in his house safe and just for him.

"I bet you don't lose your temper too often," he said with a sudden flash of insight where she was concerned. She was cool as a cucumber on the outside because Willow didn't like to let anyone know what was going on inside.

"Why do you say that?" she asked.

He waited until the waiter had put down their coffees and then left. Finding the real woman was way harder than he'd originally thought it would be. "Because you like to be in charge."

"That bothers you, doesn't it?" she asked.

He didn't want to admit it out loud but they both knew he liked being the boss. He didn't want a woman who was making him feel too much to have any control over him. But the sad fact of the matter was that whether he admitted it out loud or not, Willow was in the driver's seat.

"Yes," he said. "I like to call the shots. I was the quarterback. I'm the host and producer of my own show. I'm the master of my own destiny except where you are concerned."

"Good. You are too big for your britches," she said. "You need someone to else to challenge you. If I didn't, you'd already be bored and out the door. On to the next partner in your journey."

Her words struck him deep inside and he wondered if she wasn't right. He wanted to talk to her more about it, but he saw a group of teenagers looking at him.

Damn.

They walked over to the table and stood there for a second. "So are you Jack Crown?"

"Why, yes he is," Willow said, arching both eyebrows at him.

"Can we get your autograph?" one of them asked.

"And maybe a picture?" another asked.

"Dude, no one is going to believe this. I just saw that show last night where you did a jump on that dirt bike and got some seriously crazy air," one kid said. "How'd you do that?"

Willow just sat back and seemed to sink into the background as he signed autographs and posed for pictures. He felt her slipping further away from him and he wished he knew what to do to stop it. Had he been pushing everyone away because they acquiesced too easily? Did he want Willow because she wasn't like that? He'd have to think about it later but he doubted that anything was going to make sense to him tonight. Willow had once again shown him a new side not only to herself but also to him.

Willow had caught a cab home after the autograph-seekers had left and he hadn't blamed her. They'd kind of put a damper on the mood plus a part of him knew she needed to go home and process everything from the past.

He didn't know what to expect when he showed up to work at *Sexy & Single* the next day. Peter was standing off to one side talking with the crewman who was putting on his microphone and once they were done Jack went over to him.

"How's it going?"

"Good. I still can't believe I'm on a reality dating show," Peter said.

"I guess it's a lot different than the life you're used to," Jack said.

"Hell, yeah. Normally I travel each week to another city, get my car set up, drive as fast as I can and then do it all over again. This isn't like giving press interviews."

"You're doing good at it," Jack said.

"Well, I know how to play it for the cameras but I'm not so sure that I'm doing good with Deidre," Peter said. "She wants to take everything so slowly. It's just not in my nature to take my time, you know?"

Jack shrugged. "It's not my way to try to bond with anyone."

"Truly? Don't you get lonely?" Peter asked. "I signed

up with Matchmakers, Inc. because I just don't have time in my schedule to meet someone, and I want a family."

Jack had never thought about a family. He'd been too busy working like a madman to make sure his future was secure. And now he didn't know how to do anything else. Sure, he had fun and took vacations but he was always thinking about getting back to work. "I don't have time for a family."

"Dude, I'm racing almost every week and traveling all year long except for a break from November to the beginning of January. If I have time then you certainly do," Peter said. "Maybe you just don't want to make time or you haven't met the right woman."

"Perhaps. I do know that finding the right mate is harder than it looks," Jack said.

"So I'm not the only one to have problems with their mate?" Peter asked. "I mean, she's perfect for me, but convincing her of that is hard."

Jack laughed and clapped Peter on the shoulder. "Women are like that. And I haven't seen one couple on this show who didn't have to deal with something."

"Good to know," Peter said.

"Okay, guys," Willow said, walking over to them. "Let's get ready to shoot. Jack, I need you to ask Peter about the date planned for today and then when you lead him over to Deidre get them both talking before you move out of frame."

"No problem, boss lady," he said. He couldn't believe how she was acting this morning. Like they'd never slept together. Like he'd never seen her naked or felt her intimately pressed against him. He knew she was trying to force them back to where they had been before but he wasn't about to let her.

He snagged her hand when she started to turn away

and she glared down at his hand before jerking hers free. "We are on a tight schedule. There's a storm heading toward us. We need to get the outdoor shots before you move inside for the wine tasting."

Jack had no choice but to watch her walk away. He knew she was going to keep trying to boss him around in every aspect of their lives together. He would find an opportunity to deal with her later.

It was time Ms. Willow Stead realized who she was messing with.

"Okay, Jack, go."

Jack and Peter started walking toward the terrace where Deidre waited. "Peter, what are you looking forward to on this date today?"

"I'm hoping to show Deidre that I'm more than just a Southern boy who only knows how to drive fast."

"And how do you plan to do that?" Jack asked, knowing that it involved the wine tasting.

"I'm one of the owners of the vineyard and I think having her see me in this element will help her impression of me," Peter said.

"What do you think, Deidre? Is this what you need to see a different side of Peter?" Jack asked.

"I think so, Jack. He's certainly surprised me more than once."

"What has been the most surprising thing?" Jack asked.

"The fact that he is completely fearless when he sees something he wants. I always have to make a plan and a backup plan, but not Peter. He just goes for it."

"That's right. I can clean up the mess I make later but if I wait too long I might miss my opportunity."

"I'll get out of the way so you two can enjoy your date," Jack said, moving out of frame. The cameraman,

Willow and the rest of the crew followed them into the restaurant where the tasting was set up. Jack stood outside watching everything that was going on and letting Peter's advice settle into his head. Maybe he was going to miss something important if he didn't go after Willow now. If he'd learned anything from PJ's accident it was that life was short.

"Jack Crown?"

He turned to see a couple of kids standing to his left.

"Hey there," he said.

They came over and he signed autographs and chatted with them. But he kept his eye on Willow and he saw her watching him, too. No matter how immune she pretended to be he knew that she wasn't. She was as confused by him as he was by her.

And while he knew that one of them was going to have to give ground to move forward he didn't think it was going to be him.

Ten

Willow had another restless night sleeping in a bed that still smelled of Jack. She sort of regretted giving him the cold shoulder at work, but not really. She was tempted to pretend she hadn't slept with him.

He made it difficult for her to remember that she wasn't looking for forever with him. Hell, he'd as much as said more than once that forever wasn't in the cards for him and still she was mooning over him and having hot dreams about him. So she was cranky when she arrived at the helipad and saw Kat and Peter laughing together.

She was annoyed by it. Probably because she was in an ornery mood from yesterday's shoot and the fact that things seemed to be going great in everyone else's life. Plus, she'd warned Kat that Peter was spoken for but every time she saw her assistant she was flirting with the man. Maybe it was the lack of sleep or maybe it was her own insecurities about Jack and every other man on the planet but she just snapped.

"Kat, get over here."

Kat glanced at her with a shocked look then said something to Peter before joining Willow. Deidre hadn't arrived yet so as far as Willow was concerned this didn't have to be an issue for the couple.

"What are you doing?" Willow asked.

"Talking to the cast. Do you need me to get you some coffee?" Kat asked. "You seem out of sorts this morning."

"I'm fine. It looked like you were flirting with him. I thought I told you not to do that."

"Hey, the guy came over to me," Kat said. "It's just harmless teasing. I think he really is falling for Deidre."

Willow took a deep breath. "All the more reason for you to stay away from him. Deidre has vulnerabilities like every other woman."

"Some women like a challenge to keep their man. It makes them step up their game and go after a guy," Kat said. "You know she's been dragging her feet where he's concerned."

"So you thought you'd stoke the fire and see what comes out of it?" Willow asked. She had known Kat for a long time and knew her to be as dedicated to her career as Willow was. But then again, Willow had been spending a lot of time lately thinking about Jack when she should be focused on work. So was it fair that she was being hard on Kat?

"Sort of. He is fun and I do like him," Kat said.

Willow was about to let Kat have it when she turned to her with a sad look in her gray eyes. "What's wrong with me, Willow?"

"What do you mean?"

"The only guys I feel safe flirting with are taken. It's not like Peter's the first one I've been attracted to."

Willow put her arm around her assistant. Sometimes it was nice to know she wasn't the only one with screwed up relationship skills. "It probably feels safe to you because you know it can't go beyond flirting."

Kat pursed her lips as she considered that fact and then she nodded. "You're right. A part of me doesn't want a man messing with my life plans."

"I know the feeling," Willow said. She was never going to adjust to Jack and his presence in her life.

"Do you still feel like that?" Kat asked. "With your friends getting married and settling down, don't you want what they have?"

"No," Willow said. She almost believed her own lie but she knew that the more couple things that her friends did the more she started craving a little of what they had. But then she remembered Nichole hitting rock bottom and crying her eyes out in her apartment because Conner couldn't commit to her. Despite the fact that Conner and Nichole had worked out their issues, Willow decided maybe she was fine where she was. "I've got the good life."

"Yes, you do," Kat said. "I'll stay away from Peter from now on. I don't want to mess things up for him or for Deidre."

"Thanks," Willow said. "I don't want to have to warn you again."

"You won't have to. I like this job too much to screw up over a flirt," Kat said. She gave Willow a mock salute as she turned away.

Kat went to talk to the sound and camera guys who'd be taking a second chopper out to the Hamptons. Willow wanted to believe she was happy but a big part of her knew that she'd just gotten into the habit of coasting through life. She was content most days or she had been before Jack had shown back up.

She couldn't really blame him because he hadn't done anything to make her reevaluate where she was. But last night when they'd talked about the past she had come to understand she had always been ready to see the worst in her small town and the people in it. It in no way excused Jack for standing her up. She doubted she'd ever really be able to forget it, but she did know that her mom had acted to protect her. Willow was the only one who knew how deeply her father had hurt her mom when he'd left them.

Jack had scared her back then and no matter how much she thought she'd changed he still scared her. She caught a glimpse of him as he walked onto the roof with Deidre and she realized that that was still true.

That was why she was in such a bad mood this morning. She was attracted to a man who made her feel things she didn't want to. And the worst part was that no matter what common sense told her she wanted to run to him and wrap her arms around him. She wanted to hold on to him and make him hers. Which was stupid because Jack Crown wasn't a forever kind of guy.

Her bet with Nichole was to ensure that she could move on to someone else. Jack smiled over at her and it was all she could do to keep from frowning at him. She realized that she had to keep their relationship secret from the crew because when this ended—and she knew now that it would—she didn't want everyone to know they'd ever been together.

With that in mind she called Kat over and told her to get the talent into their chopper and have them start heading out to the Hamptons.

"Aren't you riding with them?" Kat said.

"No. I want to talk to the crew. Send hair and makeup with them," Willow said.

"Okay. I wasn't going to volunteer," Kat said a bit defensively.

"I know. I am cranky today, Kat. Sorry if I came down too hard on you," Willow said. They were cramming in as many dates as they could so they could wrap this session up before Christmas. She really couldn't have picked a worse time to get involved with Jack.

"You didn't. I needed to hear that," Kat said. "What do you need to hear?"

"That love makes women stupid," Willow said, and realized she should remember that. Was there a single woman in the world who hadn't second-guessed herself when she started a relationship with a man? She doubted it.

"Whoa, boss, when did you fall in love?" Kat asked.

Willow blanched. Had she really said that? She wasn't in love with Jack. Hell, no, she thought. Jack Crown was her ticket to the future, not a guy she was planning to be with for any length of time. "I haven't."

But she walked away from Kat feeling like those words were a lie. Had she fallen in love with Jack? No. She wouldn't let herself be that vulnerable.

Jack saw that Willow had reinforced her defenses during the night and was back to giving him the cold shoulder. He almost let her get away with it but then decided he'd had enough of waiting for Willow. It wasn't in his nature to be as tentative as he'd been with her.

And he wasn't going to be that way any longer. He signaled to Kat and told her to ride with the talent; he was riding with Willow. Willow definitely didn't look pleased when he sat down next to her and put on his headphones, but he didn't mind. He'd had the entire night to think about her and what he wanted.

"I needed Kat to ride in here so I could give her some direction before we landed."

"What could you possibly need to tell her that couldn't wait until we were on the ground? It's not exactly like this shoot will be any different than the other ones," Jack said.

"Stuff, Jack. I needed to tell her stuff and since I'm her boss—"

"You're acting like a brat," he said.

"I know. I didn't sleep well last night and have been stomping around like Godzilla all morning."

He chuckled at the way she said it. "You should have—"

She reached up and covered his mouth, giving him a warning look from her eyes. "I should have slept better, I know."

"Um…okay. Why are you acting so—" he paused, trying to find the right words "—weird?"

"I don't want to have this conversation on the chopper," she said.

"Then text me," he said.

She pulled out her cell phone and started typing a message. She handed the phone to him a second later.

I don't want anyone to know you and I are dating, she'd written.

God, this woman was going to be the death of him. Why couldn't he have become obsessed with someone who would just blindly go along with whatever he suggested? He typed a note back to her.

Nichole knows.

She rolled her eyes, typing furiously on the touch

screen. I mean at work. It will just make things complicated. So just act like we are still whatever we were.

No, he typed back.

No? I'm not playing around about this, Jack.

Too bad, Willow. I am not going to pretend that we are simply colleagues when I know we are lovers.

See? she typed. Who uses the word lovers?

I do. Is that what's bothering you? he asked.

I don't want them to talk about me when you go back to L.A. and your life and it becomes clear I was your latest booty call, she typed.

First of all booty calls aren't as complicated as you are and I'm not planning on going back to my old life.

What are you planning?

I'm not sure because as you pointed out we've only been dating for about a week. But this is more than a fling.

Technically this is week two.

Yes it is.

She put her phone away when he handed it back to her and he realized how complex she was. She acted like the opinions of others didn't matter to her yet she was afraid for everyone involved with the show to know they were a couple.

He was afraid of that, too. He didn't want to be another man that didn't measure up in Willow's eyes. He'd heard the talk on the set that she was a man-eater but he'd seen behind that reputation to the girl—scratch that, woman—who was just trying to protect herself.

They landed and Willow left his side immediately to start directing people on where they needed to go and what they needed to do. Once they were at the toy store he saw that a crowd had already arrived and he was proud to be part of this event. It was nice to be part of a show that gave back, especially at the holidays.

Peter immediately went to the people waiting who had race memorabilia in their hands and started autographing and talking to the crowd. Jack glanced over at Willow and she nodded that he should do the same. "Keep them happy."

"Will that make you happy?" he asked.

"Do you really care about that?" she asked.

"Willow, it's all I think about. You are a difficult woman to figure out."

"I know. If it makes you feel any better you're just as confusing."

"It doesn't," he said.

He walked over to talk to the crowd. There were kids with footballs and people who asked him about PJ and he realized that this was what Willow was hoping to avoid. He had gotten used to talking about his life in platitudes and quips but she knew that one day she'd be answering questions about him and Willow didn't have any artifice.

She'd tell everyone exactly how she felt. That was why she'd wanted revenge on him because she didn't have layers to protect herself. She just shot from the hip when she got backed into a corner.

Deidre came over to Peter, and Jack saw the other man stop talking to his fans to put his arm around her. He started introducing her to the crowd as they collected toys. It was then that Jack realized the cameras were running.

Willow stood over behind the cameras and Jack knew he had to do his part. He approached the couple.

"Deidre, did you imagine this Speed Racer would have a side like this?" Jack asked.

"Not at first. But the man I've gotten to know really cares about people," she said, giving Peter an intimate smile.

"I certainly do and I'm not afraid to let the world know it," Peter said.

"I'm beginning to understand why," Deidre said. "I guess when you feel something that intensely you have to let it out."

Jack didn't know how to respond to that. It was the opposite of what was going on between him and Willow. They were both trying to contain whatever they felt and he thought maybe that was a mistake. But he wasn't too sure.

He only knew that in order for him to be happy with Willow he was going to have to do something to shake things up. The way he had the other night. He couldn't let her keep him at arm's length at work because she'd just keep doing that in their real lives as well. And watching Deidre, who'd been so afraid to be publicly hurt by Peter, hold his hand and let the world see she'd fallen for him gave Jack the courage to do the same.

Willow was in a much better mood when she arrived at the MacAfee family's house in the Hamptons. Conner used it when he wanted to get away from the city for the weekend. According to Nichole, this was where she'd crashed a party on the Fourth of July and gotten her first audience with Conner.

The house was decorated for fall with a large wreath on the door and brown, orange and yellow flower arrangements scattered throughout. She and Jack had come over together and he stood in the foyer with her.

"This is living," Jack said. "I really like this place. I've been looking for a house on the East Coast. My apartment is too small if I'm going to be spending more than a week there."

"Thanks. My mom spends more time out here than I do. I think one of the women on her tennis team is a Realtor. I'll get her information for you," Conner said, coming to greet them. "It was the one house that Mom brought to the marriage with my father. It came down from her grandparents. You wouldn't know it to look at it but originally it was just a little cottage."

"It's beautiful," Willow said.

"Nic is in the living room. She hasn't been feeling well today," Conner said.

"Should we leave?" Willow asked, worried for her friend. Nichole hadn't planned to get pregnant but from the moment she had realized she was she'd wanted her baby. "What's wrong?"

"Apparently I'm not a very sensitive man," Conner said.

Willow shook her head, slightly relieved that it was nothing more than something Conner had said. But it was hard to believe that a couple as right for each other as Nichole and Conner would be fighting. "What'd you say?"

"That she wouldn't be fat forever."

"Oh, no," Willow said, fighting back a smile.

"In my defense she was lamenting she would be," Conner said with a shrug of his big shoulders. And Willow caught a glimpse of the panic in his eyes.

"I think she wanted you to say she wasn't fat," Jack said, giving advice man-to-man. "Right, Willow?"

"I got that but it's too late. She's banned me from the living room."

"I'll go chat with her and see if I can get her to change her mind," Willow said.

"Sounds like a plan. Want to see my newest toy?" Conner asked Jack. "It's a fast car that Alex Cannon told me about."

Willow left the men and headed toward the living room where she found Nichole sitting on a large leather sofa with a pashmina around her shoulders. Her friend looked tired and beautiful. Not fat at all.

"Hey there. You okay?" Willow asked as she walked into the room and sat down on the couch next to Nichole.

"No. I'm not in control of my body or my hormones and I keep saying stupid things," Nichole said. "No one ever told me that being pregnant equaled losing IQ points."

Willow gave her a one-armed hug. "What's this really about? Conner knows you're not stupid."

"Yes, he does. But lately I'm just tired and swollen and cranky all the time. I thought I'd be one of those women who glow while she's pregnant. Instead I feel like a mess. And you know Conner—he always looks so sophisticated and cool and I just…I'm feeling sorry for myself."

Willow shook her head. "Um, you married one of the wealthiest men in America and he is totally devoted to you. You are about to have a baby—something Gail can't ever do—and you have a career you love. Yeah, life is tough for you, Nic."

"I told you I was being whiny."

"I know. I was a bitch this morning," Willow said. "We can't be perfect all the time."

"So true. Glad I'm not the only one out of sorts today. Maybe we can blame it on the alignment of the stars," Nichole said. "Am I closer to winning my spa day?"

"Closer than I want you to be. He's not an ass," Willow said.

Nichole laughed and shook her head. "We already knew that. So what has he done lately?"

"Just apologized for the past," Willow said. "I didn't think he'd do that but he was so sincere and I just couldn't stay mad about it when he did it."

"That's good. That's progress, even if nothing else comes of this. Do you feel better now?"

"No," Willow admitted. "I'm still me. I'm still afraid to let him get close, and the harder I try to keep him at bay the more he slips past my barriers. And he won't do what I tell him to."

"Good."

"What? I thought you were on my side," Willow said.

"I am. But you need someone to shake things up for you. You are in a rut and it's not doing you any good."

"Yes, but I'm safe, Nic. Really safe. No one has broken my heart in years and as much as I might miss the closeness I see between you and Conner, it's a lot safer my way."

"What could come between you and Jack?"

"A million things. For one—he lives on the West Coast."

"That's a nonissue. You work in the same industry and if you had to move it wouldn't be the end of the world," Nichole said.

"I'd miss you," she said.

"I'd visit you lots. I'm just saying that's not a deal breaker. But something is a deal breaker for you or you wouldn't be putting up this many barriers. What is it?"

Willow tried to think what it was she really was afraid of with Jack. She didn't think it could be as simple as just not wanting to get her heart broken. That was silly. But on the other hand she thought it might be.

There was something about Jack that had always made him seem to be out of her league.

Did she still not feel like she was good enough for him? Was it that part of her was embarrassed about where she'd come from? Not the place but her people?

"I just don't know," Willow said.

"Until you figure that out, you're going to keep putting obstacles in your own way. And you won't be happy," Nichole said.

"Well, it's not that easy," Willow said.

"I know. Remember when you and Gail came to my apartment and found me moping in the living room with the Keurig and romantic movies? Because I thought it was over with Conner?"

"Yes. What's your point?"

"I had to confront my demons and figure out what I was afraid to lose. Conner wasn't going to let me in if I kept trying to force him. I had to make peace with the fact that I might lose. I might have to walk away. And in walking away he decided he didn't want to let me go. That was a huge step."

"I don't know if I can take a risk like that."

Nichole gave her a sad smile. "Your future happiness depends on it."

Eleven

By the time they got back to the city, it was almost night. A light snow was falling and the neighborhood kids were playing outside under the glow of the streetlamp. It had snowed maybe once a year in the North Dallas suburb where Willow had grown up and she remembered doing the same thing. It didn't usually snow this much in New York in November, either, but the weather like everything else in her life wasn't predictable this year.

"Remember the snowball fight we had?" Jack said. "You had a very strong arm for someone who wasn't an athlete."

She shook her head. "Well, I did get advice from the best arm in the state that year. You helped me out."

"Yes, I did. And you repaid me by hitting me in the back of the head."

She chuckled as she remembered that. "I know you

won't believe it but it was luck. I was aiming for your back."

She unlocked her door and then turned to look back at him. She wasn't sure what she was going to do next. He looked unsure, and that wasn't like Jack. But then neither of them was behaving true to form. He stood in the doorway of her brownstone and Willow was this close to sending him away before she just reached out and grabbed his hand, bringing him into her house.

"We need to talk." Today had shown her that if she wasn't careful everyone in her life was going to know she and Jack were dating…and had slept together. It was ironic, even to her, that she who'd pried into other couples' relationships wanted to keep her own private.

"Uh-oh. That doesn't sound good. I guess I'm not coming in to warm your bed."

She ignored that as she walked down the hall to her living room. She didn't want to think about a sexy naked Jack in her bed. But too late—the image was planted in her mind and she couldn't shake it.

Jack followed her, his footsteps heavy on the hardwood floor. Willow wasn't sure what she was going to say but knew that if she didn't get this part of her life under control, the rest of it was going to be a mess.

"We really need to be—" she started and then stopped. He put his hands in the pockets of his jeans and tipped his head to the side, smiling at her. "You are making me crazy," she said.

"That's only fair since you've been doing the exact same thing to me since we met on the set of *Sexy & Single*. You think that I'm the problem but it all boils down to you, more or less."

"Not true. You were just asking me out to begin with because I said no."

He nodded. "Fair enough. I was doing it to needle you because you just kept looking through me. No man wants to be invisible."

"Especially not one as visible as you," she said.

"Not fair. I can't control how other people act when I'm out. And I apologized for that scene at the coffee house. You know that's not how I am," Jack said. "I'm just an average guy."

"You're not average and you never have been," she said. From the first moment she'd met him, he'd been the golden boy. "Even in high school you were destined for fame. You know that's true."

He looked uncomfortable but he didn't deny it. "It doesn't change the fact that I'm a man who has spent his life trying to…"

"What?"

"I don't know. I think I've been trying to just keep moving."

And those words were Jack. He might have sent her a frog prince but she knew deep inside that if she kissed him and turned him into a prince he wouldn't know how to react. Jack was used to moving along.

"Moving on," she said, softly to herself. She wished the words could mean more to her heart than they did but she'd figured out earlier today that they didn't. She liked him way more than was sensible.

Everything about him was a warning but instead of heeding it, she was running headlong into the one thing—the one relationship—that she really couldn't control.

"Why is that a problem?" he asked.

She shrugged and turned away from him to look at the comfortable living room where she'd created a safe little nest for herself. It was the one place in the world where she felt at home. And she'd brought him here. Why did she keep doing that?

"Willow?"

What could she say?

"I want to force us back to where we used to be so I can pretend you didn't see me naked with all my emotional warts visible."

He walked over to her and pulled her into his arms. "I was the same way. We have to decide…are we dating? And if we are then there isn't going to be any hiding it. We just do this like a normal couple would."

"What's normal?" she asked because she remembered Gail, who'd been set up for six dates with Russell on the show, learning that his ex-girlfriend was pregnant and having to deal with that. She also remembered Nichole having to barter with Conner and risk herself. Risk, she thought, suddenly. The key to her friends' happiness had come from really putting themselves on the line.

That was what Nichole had been trying to tell her earlier. And Willow didn't know if she could do that.

"Normal is whatever we come up with. For me I want what PJ and Rhia have. And what the couples on our show are searching for. Is that too much to ask?"

It wasn't. She was beginning to believe that no one had an easy go at relationships. Which would make sense since she'd seen the numbers on viewers for her show. People were tuning in in droves to watch other couples make mistakes and if Willow had to guess she'd say they were looking for answers the same way she was.

"No," she said, pushing away from him. "It's not. But that doesn't make it any easier. I mean, we could be totally wrong for each other in the long run."

"There is no long run," he said. "There is just right now."

She pushed away from him and realized that the risk she was taking was bigger than she'd realized but she'd never been a coward and walking away from Jack wasn't an option. She wanted to see this through to the end and not because of a bet, but because it was Jack, and she honestly couldn't walk away from him. Not until he did something that pushed her too far.

The fact that that was an option in the back of her head should have told her something but she refused to believe it tonight. Tonight she just wanted to have him hold her and pretend she didn't know that there were no easy paths to happiness. Tonight she wanted to make believe that they could be together forever.

She almost laughed out loud at that thought. The man who didn't think anything could last—he could never be her forever man. He couldn't.

Maybe if she repeated it enough times she'd be able to convince herself of that.

Jack felt like Willow was slipping away from him, so he did the one thing that he knew would keep her closer to him, at least for tonight. He swept her up in his arms and carried her down the hallway to her bedroom. He'd thought of nothing else but getting back into her bed since he'd left it.

"What's this?"

"You're a smart woman, Willow. I think you know what this is."

"I do," she said. "But I'm not sure this is the answer."

"Hell, this is the only thing we have between us that is right. I don't want to go back to my cold lonely apartment but if you say you want me to..."

"I don't want you to. I've missed you. Each night I sleep on sheets that still hold the scent of your after-shave."

"Good."

"Good?" she asked.

"Yes, I've been tortured with images of you and your naked body wrapped around mine night after night. I'm glad you've had the same problem sleeping that I have."

She pushed on his chest and he fell back on her bed. He scooted up toward the headboard and piled the pillows behind his back. Willow stood there at the end of the bed for a minute then slowly pulled her sweater over her head. Her long hair fanned out around her shoulders as she tossed it aside.

"Do me a favor?"

"What?"

"Take off your bra and pull your hair forward over your breasts," he said.

She nodded and did what he asked. He groaned and hardened in his jeans. She did a little shimmy and removed her pants, bending over to take off her shoes. Then she stood there naked draped only with her own hair.

She proudly let him look his fill at her luscious body. Then she climbed onto the bed and started to work her way up toward him. She straddled his hips and brought her mouth down to his. She guided his hands, and he rubbed them all over her naked body. Her skin was so soft and warm, and he couldn't get enough of touching her.

She sat back on his thighs and pulled his sweater up and over his head, tossing it aside. Then she did the same thing with his T-shirt.

"I like your chest," she said, running her fingers over the heavy pads of his muscles.

"I like yours, too," he said, cupping her breasts and pinching her nipples lightly. She shifted forward and put her hands on the back of his head, drawing his mouth to her breast. He licked one nipple and then drew it into his mouth, sucking strongly at her and feeling like he was about to explode.

She moaned and rocked her pelvis back and forth over his hard-on, which was still trapped in the fabric of his jeans. He took control of her hips, rubbing her against his erection where he liked the sensation of her.

She pulled back when he lifted his head, smiling down at him. She knew she had him in the palm of her hand and Willow liked it. To be honest, he liked it, too.

She undid his jeans and he lifted his hips so she could draw them down his legs. She took care of his shoes and socks before pushing all the articles to the floor. Then she caressed her way back up his body, stopping to linger over his injured knee.

It was scarred and ugly. Even though it had been more than ten years, the scars were still visible and always would be. The kind of surgery he'd had left marks. And to be honest Jack had always thought that there should be a permanent reminder of something that had been so life changing.

"Does it still hurt?" she asked.

"Not usually. If I do something stupid, it does," he said.

She leaned down and kissed each scar gently. Her fingers caressed his thigh muscles and he had to admit that he stopped thinking when he felt the brush of the back of her fingers against him. His hips jerked forward involuntarily and he reached down to take a handful of Willow's hair.

It was soft, and as she turned her head the long strands caressed him. Then she shifted so she knelt between his legs and she smiled up at him as she stroked his erection. The sexual teasing had gone on long enough. He was hot for her and he needed to be back inside her warm silky body. He felt cold without her. He didn't want to admit how much he needed her.

He wanted to pretend that it was just sexual, that he needed the orgasm she'd give him, but he needed more than that. He pulled her up his body but she resisted, dropping kisses and nibbles on his body as he tried to force her up. He felt the brush of her tongue on the tip of his hard-on and everything in him tightened.

He reached for her hips as her mouth engulfed the tip of him and fondled her, finding her wet and ready for him. He caressed her bud as she tongued him and he wanted to stay caught in this tender moment forever. But his blood was starting to boil and he needed more than just her mouth on him.

He pulled his hips away from her and came around behind her. She leaned forward putting her hands on the top of the headboard as he nudged her thighs apart and adjusted his hips.

She shifted forward and canted her hips up and backward toward him. He waited until they were both desperate for it. Then he cupped both of her breasts and leaned over her neck to bite the base of it as he drew back his hips and thrust as deep as he could into her.

He drove into her again and again and she rocked back taking each of his thrusts and calling out his name as he pounded a rhythm that drove them both to the brink of orgasm and then finally over into it. He was shaking and held on to her with all of his strength as the last of his essence left his body. He cradled her to him as he rolled onto his side and pulled her closer, hugging her to him. He buried his head in her hair and the warm curve of her neck.

He knew without a doubt that this had solved nothing but he felt a sense of peace and for just tonight he believed that he would be holding Willow in his arms not just for the foreseeable future but also for the next fifty years.

But damn, that thought scared him—and made him realize it was past time for him to leave.

A week later, there was magic to the night, with the lights of Rockefeller Center all around them. The fall night was brisk and cold but no snow fell. Willow stood on the edge of the ice skating rink watching both Deidre and Peter try to make their way around the rink hand in hand. She got a little choked up.

"They look good together," Jack said, coming up next to her.

She had been trying to avoid him at work because she didn't really want everyone to know that they'd slept together. Hell. she didn't want to admit to herself that she'd given in and fallen for his charms.

Except he wasn't that shallow player she'd first thought he was. He was a complex man who genuinely cared about others, and she wanted so much to believe that what they had could last…even though that very thought made her realize it never could. She wanted it too much. She'd do something to ruin it the way she always did.

"They do," she squeaked, then winced. Why was

it that when she experienced emotions and Jack at the same time, she turned into a child's squeaky toy?

"You okay?"

"Yes, I think I might be getting a cold," she said, hoping he'd buy that instead of realizing that she was sad thinking about the fact that Thanksgiving was only a few days away. They'd be filming the last week's date soon and Jack wouldn't have a reason to stay here with her.

"Want to give it a try?" he asked.

"Ice skating?"

"Yes, Willow, ice skating," he said.

"I don't know how. I've never done it."

"Why not? You live in New York."

"I grew up in Texas," she said. "At a certain point in my life I decided that things like walking on hard ice weren't smart."

"Scaredy cat."

"Oh, that's really mature," she said, but his goad had worked. She hated to be called names. Even if they were true. And she knew she was scared of everything that had to do with Jack. She had been since…since she'd first met him that long ago afternoon in the school library. She'd been sure he'd break her heart and, low and behold, he had.

"Do you know how?"

"Of course. There's nothing I can't do," he said, but with a sweet sexy smile.

"Will you make sure I don't fall?"

"Willow, I'll protect you with my life if I have to."

Part of her knew he was saying it to be silly but another part of her—that sweet innocent girl she protected deep inside of herself—that girl melted into a puddle. "Okay, I'll do it."

"Good. Kat, go and get us some skates. Willow and I are going skating."

"Yes, sir," Kat said, giving Willow a curious look.

Willow knew that tomorrow her assistant was going to be full of questions about why she'd gone ice-skating with Jack. Hell, she knew that Kat was smart enough to be able to figure out that she and Jack were…what? Dating? Sleeping together?

This was it. The thing she couldn't handle. She made some mumbled excuse and turned away from him and the couples skating around the ice. She moved to a darkened corner where she could be alone but Jack was there.

He put his hands on her shoulders and rubbed them. "What are you afraid of?"

"You."

"Ah, Willow, how am I supposed to remember you're in charge of everything when you say things like that?"

"But control is an illusion, isn't it? The longer I'm with you the more I see that I'm not in charge of anything."

"Neither of us is," he said, pulling her back against his chest and wrapping his arms around her. He turned them so they faced the ice rink and she saw all the couples making their way around the circle. He leaned his chin against her shoulder. "They aren't in control, either. Life could change in an instant for any of them. Hell, Peter could have an accident the next time he gets behind the wheel of a car, but Deidre is still taking a chance on him, on letting him in."

"I know. She's brave to do that."

"Everyone is. We can't live our lives alone. I don't know why but it just doesn't work when we try it."

"Well, not for you because you have legions of fans," she said, but she knew he'd meant someone special.

"Don't be a brat, Willow. You know I meant you. If you want to pretend that you're nothing more than just another woman to me, then you do that. But you are stealing a chance at something precious from both of us."

"Do I really have that kind of power over you?" she asked.

"Yes. And I suspect I have it over you. That's why you keep backing away. That's why you say you have to be in charge. You're hoping that by calling all the shots you won't be as vulnerable but it's too late for that.

"I suspect it was too late from the very moment we met. Fate has put us in each other's path again because we have unfinished business together," he continued.

"You sound very wise, Jack. I'm not sure I buy that. You're the man who told me nothing lasts forever. Am I just a road bump on your journey?"

"No," he said, leaning over to kiss the side of her cheek, his lips warm against her cold skin. "You're my partner on this part of the journey. I hope it lasts a long time because I really get a kick out of having you by my side. But I don't know what the future holds and neither do you."

That didn't reassure her but she suspected he hadn't meant for it to. That wasn't the way that Jack was.

"Tonight we have a chance to do something that is romantic together and I don't want to miss it," he said. "So will you stop worrying and go skating with me?"

She turned in his arms and kissed him just because she could and as he'd said, who knew how long they'd have together? Why not enjoy the moments they did have?

"Yes."

Twelve

Willow felt like she and Jack were closer than ever as they drove to Nichole and Conner's for Thanksgiving. He'd done an appearance on NBC for their coverage of the Macy's Thanksgiving Day Parade and now they were on their way to the penthouse apartment in Midtown.

The car that Jack had hired was a nice big comfortable sedan that provided a warm safe haven from the cold crowded streets. He looked sexy and sophisticated in his suit and tie and as he wrapped his arm around her shoulder and drew her into the curve of his body she felt like she was in the exact right place for once in her life.

His cell phone rang and he shifted to get his phone out. He glanced at the caller ID and then took his arm from around her shoulder and canted his body away from hers as he answered it.

"Crown here."

She tried not to listen in but it was impossible being

as close as she was to him. "Thanks, Rhia. I'm going to be in New York until Sunday. I'll come by the hospital as soon as I land."

He hung up a few minutes later but she was still dealing with the fact that he was leaving in three days time and he hadn't mentioned it to her. It seemed like pushing past barriers and having her be honest was a one-way street. Not that she should have been too surprised. Jack had a busy schedule and they'd scarcely had a moment alone together since their ice-skating date a few days ago.

"So you're heading back to L.A. after we finish taping?"

"Yes. I put off *Extreme Careers* as long as I could. We took a little break to wait for PJ to recover. They want to get the season in the can and I have to tape a post-attack interview with him."

"Why didn't you mention it?"

"It doesn't really concern us," Jack said.

"What do you mean? Of course it does. You said we'd be like a normal couple. Couples talk to each other and tell each other when they are going out of town."

He sighed, rubbed the back of his neck and turned to face her. "You're right. I've been avoiding it because I don't really want to leave you, Willow. And I didn't want to say that to you."

"Why not?" she asked, trying not to smile from the happiness that had bloomed inside of her. She felt a hell of a lot better because he'd uttered those few words. She knew that was a mistake. She had to be the captain of her happiness but for today she didn't want to think about that.

"Because you keep everything you feel bottled up deep inside and I'm the one who's bumbling around in the dark hoping that you're falling for me the way I'm falling for you. But I don't know if that's happening. And that scares me, Willow. You scare me more than that shark did when it attacked PJ."

She sank back away from him and realized that this was the moment she'd been hoping for back when she'd accepted Nichole's bet. She had Jack on the ropes and she could deliver the knockout punch with just a few well-chosen words but she knew if she did that she'd spend the rest of her life regretting it.

"You scare me, too," she said, her voice small and quiet even to her own ears. "Every time I think I can manage you and the feelings you evoke in me, you do something else to jar me out of my comfort zone and my illusion of control."

"Glad to know I'm not the only one."

"That doesn't really make it any better. Just gives us company in our misery."

"Except I haven't felt miserable," Jack said. "Not while I've been with you. Is it the same for you?"

She swallowed hard. Oh, God. Could she do this? Could she take the risk that if she showed him how deeply she cared for him that he'd do the same? Could she trust him? Jack Crown, the boy who'd made her afraid of trusting men…

"Uh…"

"That's what I thought. You like to see me crawl and you give me just enough rope to make me think you're on the other end but when I tug you're not there."

His words hurt her but she couldn't blame him for his anger. "I'm really not toying with you. I'm just not sure I can trust you."

"If you can't trust me then who are you going to

trust? You don't let anyone close to you, not even Gail and Nichole."

"That's not true."

"Yes, it is. Gail came to you with her idea of changing her life and instead of getting behind her and helping her out, you make a television show about her."

Willow shrank back against the seat. His words had an element of truth to them. It had been easier to make Gail's life a work project than to face the fact that her friends were moving on to a new phase she wasn't ready for.

"I didn't mean to do anything—

"Hell, I know that. I just mean you don't trust anyone to just be yourself around them. I think I'm closer to you than any other person on the planet and yet you still keep pushing me away."

Suddenly she felt like she was the one on the ropes, not Jack. And he could easily deliver the deathblow to her and her secret hopes for the future. Jack was way more than a friendly face that she'd gotten used to seeing and she knew that she'd been hoping that she could find a way to kiss him and keep him.

"I don't do it intentionally. It's just that I don't know how to show you that I want you to stay. Then if you decide to leave…how will I carry on? It seems easier for me to deal with if I never admit that you have that power over me."

He reached over and pulled her into his arms. "You have the same power over me. We are both out of our element here. We are two people who don't trust easily. You don't trust people to be there when you need them and I…"

He was right about that. She even guarded herself with Nichole and Gail but it was easier with them because she'd known them before she knew that caring could hurt.

"You?" she prompted.

"I'm afraid to believe that when I find someone or something that I care about that it will last."

She hugged him tight and wanted to offer promises that she'd be here by his side forever, but she didn't believe those words. She was afraid to take a chance on expressing the love that she'd been hiding from him. Because like he'd said, things didn't last for him, and the two of them had a history that didn't bode well for a super-rosy future no matter how much they both wanted it.

Neither of them said another word until they got to Nic and Conner's apartment. Jack held her hand as they rode up in the elevator but Willow was painfully aware that nothing had been settled.

Jack had spent last Thanksgiving at The Palm Hotel in Dubai, which couldn't have been more different than this year. Conner and Nichole were gracious hosts and had opened their home not just to Jack and Willow but also to Gail and Russell, Conner's sister Jane and his mother, Ruthann MacAfee, as well the South American polo player Palmer Cassini.

Jane was a lifestyle guru with her own television show, so she'd been in charge of the meal and the tablescape. Jack hadn't known what that was—apparently it involved decorating the table with stuff other than plates and cutlery. He was happy enough when Willow waved him off to the living room with the men to watch football.

He needed a break from the emotional tension brewing between him and Willow. There was too much they both had left unsaid. Sometimes he felt like they were both playing at being normal and being in a regular relationship.

Russell was a New Zealander who hadn't grown up watching football. But he had a very good grasp of it, which didn't surprise Jack since Russell was smart and moved in a world where knowledge was power.

"We never watched American football when I was growing up," Palmer said.

"In Texas we hardly watched anything else…except maybe baseball and basketball," Jack said with a grin.

"Can I get you a drink?" Conner asked from the bar on one side of the room.

"What do you have?" Jack asked.

"Well, Jane made a pitcher of what she's calling Pilgrim's Friend. It has pomegranate juice and a couple of different types of liquor in it. Palmer's been drinking it."

"How is it?"

"It's good," Palmer said.

"He's also in lust with the woman who made it and trying to get on her good side," Russell said.

"I guess I'll try it," Jack said. "I can always switch to beer later."

"Good plan," Conner said.

They settled down to watch the game. The men had a good camaraderie and included Jack in their group. He felt like he was glimpsing one version of his future. If he and Willow ended up together he could spend his holidays like this from now on instead of at an anonymous resort half a world away.

When the game went to a commercial for a coach's challenge, Jack turned to Conner and asked, "How's Nichole feeling this week?"

"Much better," Conner said. "She got a sonogram. Want to see the picture?"

Jack nodded. Russell gave him a smirk. "To think that you almost missed out on being a daddy."

"He did?" Jack asked.

"Oh, yes, Conner was determined to stay a bachelor," Palmer said.

"Whatever. You both are as hopeless as I am. Russell really screwed up," Conner said, coming back over to the couch and handing Jack a printout with a picture of his unborn child. Jack looked down at it and had a flashback to that moment when he'd seen Willow holding Bella Ann, and he realized what he should have known all along. He wanted her for the long haul. He might be afraid to say the words to her but the truth was there in his heart whether he admitted it or not.

He wanted to pretend that he was an ordinary man who was like everyone else but he never had been. And the woman he'd fallen in love with was harder to get close to than any other, but that was okay, he realized. That was what made him and Willow work together.

"Gail and I are going to try to adopt. You know I can't have kids. We thought about artificial insemination but then Gail said there are so many children out there who need to be loved. Well, it just made sense."

"That's great," Jack said.

"More than great, that's wonderful news. Nichole will be very happy to hear it. She wants Gail and Willow to have kids close in age to ours so they can all grow up as friends," Conner said.

Jack stood up and walked away as the men continued talking about kids with each other. He was almost ready to let Willow know how he felt but there was no way he was ready to think about children. Good God, life was fragile enough. Worrying about Willow was one thing—what if he had another being who counted on him? Another little person to be afraid for. He didn't think he could do it.

"Dinner's ready," Jane said from the doorway.

Jack just stared at her, afraid that if he went into that room he'd be tempted by a life that he'd never thought he wanted. It didn't make any sense to him. It scared him deep inside that getting Willow was just the first of many scary obstacles that a life with a partner would bring him up against.

"Are you okay?" Willow asked as he took his seat next to her at the long dinner table. Palmer was seated to Jane's right at the foot of the table. Nichole and Ruthann sat on either side of Conner at the other end. Gail and Russell were seated across from Jack and Willow.

The smell of turkey and all the trimmings filled the room. There were more of those cocktails of Jane's and Willow kept looking at him while he concentrated on this beautiful life that he felt like he couldn't really be a part of.

"Jack?"

"Sorry. I'm fine. Just not used to this," he said.

"I'm not, either. This is the first family Thanksgiving I've had since my mom died."

He realized in that moment that both of them had been without a home for too long and as scared as he was to gamble on the future, it made him feel a lot better to think of her by his side.

"A toast," Conner said, lifting his glass into the air. They all did the same and he took a minute to compose himself.

Jack was surprised to find himself in the inner circle of the reclusive Conner MacAfee. He held his cocktail glass in his hand and looked around at the people at the table.

“To family, friends and the many holidays that we will share,” Conner said.

“Here, here,” Russell said.

They all clinked their glasses, and Jack reached up to loosen his collar as the afternoon closed in around him. He ate the meal and kept up with the conversation on sports and predictions of which films they thought would get an Oscar nomination. But he felt removed from the room. He felt like this wasn’t real and that only once he got out of here and back to his empty apartment could he relax.

And then the strangest thing happened. Willow reached under the table and touched his thigh, rubbed it up and down and squeezed it. Then she leaned over and whispered in his ear, “I’m so glad you are here with me.”

Something melted inside of him and his fears faded. He wasn’t alone with Willow. She probably felt the same way he did. It might be even worse for her since these were her friends. This was her world that had completely changed.

Dinner was tense for Jack because he felt trapped and so emotionally laid bare by everything that it was a relief once it was over.

“Jack, I have that Realtor information I promised you. Come into the den and I’ll get it for you,” Conner said as the dessert dishes were being cleared from the table.

Jack was happy to leave the group—and Willow—for a few moments. He could see that she was enjoying herself—there was almost a glow about her as she kept looking at him and her friends. Today was some sort of perfect setting for her and for him it just felt like…well, something that couldn’t last.

He didn’t like the position he found himself in and

if he could think of a good excuse he'd be out the door in a second.

Conner's den was decorated in dark wood paneling and had a huge desk. It reminded Jack of his high school coach's den back in Texas. But then Coach Steel had been a fairly wealthy man and that had been saying something back when Jack was in Frisco.

"Nice place," Jack said.

"Thanks. I'm used to a certain level of comfort and privacy when I'm working from home," Conner said. "Being married is forcing me to change that."

"How are you finding marriage?" Jack asked. "I'm curious because you were the most confirmed bachelor I've ever met."

"Indeed I was. But my life is so much richer with Nichole. There are times when I want to run away and close the door and go back to my old habits but then Nichole will do something that makes me realize that I was simply hiding away before."

Jack wondered what that was and if Willow would be able to do the same for him but Nichole and Willow were very different. Just because Nichole could make Conner happy didn't mean Willow could do the same for him.

"How are things working out with you and Willow?" Conner asked. "You seem pretty happy with each other today."

"We are. It's hard for us because we are both workaholics who are determined to be in charge of every aspect of our lives but I think we are working it out," Jack said.

And he believed that. No matter how hard it was to get comfortable with this new arrangement he couldn't forget the reassurance he'd gotten from Willow's hand on his leg during dinner. It seemed to imply that they were a team. That they would both face these things together. And that was so tempting.

He realized that he'd wanted someone to share his life with, but had been afraid to risk caring enough for someone to let them in. Willow had snuck into his heart when he hadn't been looking and he felt like…well that she could be his partner on the journey and he was even willing to put aside his fear that she wouldn't always be by his side.

He nodded as he came to a decision—perhaps one he should have made in the car before he got here. "Yes, Willow and I are getting along very well."

"I'm happy for you. When Nic told me about the bet that she and Willow made I thought it was stupid. You can't bet on your friends' happiness, but Nic said that if she hadn't, Willow would never have gone out with you."

What? he thought. What the hell was Conner talking about? Jack used all his professional skills to keep that confusion from showing on his face.

"What were the terms of the bet?" Jack asked. "I never heard them."

"Well, Nic has won a day at the Red Door Salon thanks to you, man. You made Willow fall for you," Conner said.

Jack was enraged inside and he thought if he stayed here another second he was going to get all Hulk on not only Conner but also Willow. "Did you say you had that real estate information?"

"Oh, yes. Here's our Realtor's number. Mother also knows the owner of the place two houses down from us. She hasn't put it on the market yet but it's going up for sale soon. I think you can get a good price if you call her this weekend."

"Thanks, Conner," Jack said, taking the business card

from the other man. Then he paused. He had one more question. “How does Nic know she’s won? I mean Willow and I are still sorting things out.”

“She knows because Willow didn’t break your heart and walk out the door as she’d been planning to do from the beginning.”

“Lucky me,” Jack said. Knowing that Willow had just done it anyway. He tried to be rational and remind himself that he’d hurt her in the past. Maybe she would have mentioned the bet at some point in time if they’d talked about it. But he doubted it. He also wasn’t entirely sure that Nichole had won. Who was to say that Willow hadn’t hesitated to tell him how she felt because she wanted to make sure he was well and truly hooked?

She was someone who could wait as long as she needed to get revenge. She’d told him so. He stuffed the card into his pocket and walked out of the den to find that Gail and Russell had their coats on and were getting ready to leave.

As far as Jack was concerned that meant they could all go. He glanced over at Willow and signaled for her to get her coat. She arched one eyebrow at him and gave him a good hard glare but he was in no mood to deal with it so he shrugged.

“I’ve got to head out, too,” he said to Nichole. “Thank you both for your hospitality. Willow, are you coming with me?”

“Of course I am. Sorry for having to eat and run,” Willow said. “But Jack has to get back to work on the West Coast on Sunday so we are cramming a lot in this weekend.”

“It’s okay, I get it. He probably wants to be alone with you,” Nichole said.

Jack grinned over at both women. “I certainly do.”

Thirteen

"What the hell was that all about?" Willow asked as soon as they were in the car.

"I'd rather wait until we are at my apartment to talk," he said and turned away from her as the driver made quick time through the city to Jack's place.

He tipped the driver and thanked him for working on the holiday. They got out of the car and he held open the outer door to the building for her. It was cold and gray outside like the coldness that had settled inside Willow.

She could tell Jack was on edge as soon as they walked into his apartment. She had the feeling that dinner today hadn't made him see that they were meant to spend a life together.

"You seemed in a hurry to get out of there," she said, trying to egg him on a little so she'd know what was going on. "Did Conner say anything rude to you?"

"Nope. Sorry if you felt rushed. You could have stayed."

He was definitely in a mood. "But it was all couples."

"And Ruthann. I'm sure she would have been good company," Jack said.

"Did you talk to her about a house in the Hamptons?"

"Among other things" he said.

"Okay, are we done?" she asked. She had to know what he was saying. What exactly was going on? She'd had such a great time at dinner and had felt like she'd finally found the one man she wanted by her side.

"We were never started, were we?" he asked. "I mean I was some kind of unresolved thing from your past and you were just a woman who was a challenge."

She shook her head. "I know it was more than that to you. What happened to scare you today?"

"Nothing. I just remembered that what we saw today isn't our lives, Willow. You and me, we don't do big family gatherings. You and I are loners."

"I kind of liked it. I thought we were becoming more than loners."

He shook his head. "No, we aren't. We'd both have to stop trying to protect ourselves and let the other one in. And to be honest I'm not the kind of man who can go out on a limb by myself."

"Give me a chance, Jack. I can join you out on that limb. But I have to know—"

"You want guarantees and there aren't any. Look at our friends tonight…tomorrow something could happen to any one of them. Look at PJ and Rhia, she's lucky to still have him but he's not the same man she fell in love with. That might be enough to drive them apart."

"We aren't them. We don't take dangerous risks with our lives—well, I don't take risks. You do and I think you like it," Willow said, realizing that she wished she hadn't been so cowardly earlier. If she'd told him how she felt maybe he wouldn't have felt pushed to this point.

"No, you don't take risks, and even knowing that we were both afraid to admit we cared. I can't think of two people less likely to actually make a go at a life together than you and me. I know you said it before and I'm just agreeing with you. You are right, Willow."

But she didn't think she was. Not anymore. Why did he have to agree with her now, when she'd changed her mind? She stared at him and she knew if she confessed her feelings he'd maybe have a change of heart.

He looked fierce, though, as he stood across from her there in his loft apartment. She glanced around it remembering the first time she'd come here for dinner. Remembering all that had gone between them. She had thought that maybe he'd be the one to save her but then she was projecting her own desires onto him again. Like she had in high school.

"Fine. You're right. This was a mistake. I don't know what I was thinking."

"Maybe you were thinking that you could win the bet with Nichole," he said.

"How'd you hear about that?" she asked.

"Conner mentioned it. Thought I'd know what had motivated you to come to dinner with me."

Oh, God, this wasn't good. "What'd you say?"

"Just laughed it off. But I was thinking that it said a lot about the person you are, Willow. I keep thinking you just are afraid to tell me you care about me, but what if it's more than that? What if it's that you just want to win a bet with your friend and make me hurt the way I hurt you."

Willow wrapped her arms around her own waist and stared at him. What could she say? "That changed."

"When did it change? Because on our way to Conner and Nichole's it hadn't. And I'm pretty sure it didn't change on the way back," he said. "In fact I'm having a hard time believing that you don't want revenge on me. That you haven't been stringing me along just to drive the knife in a little deeper when the time was right."

"I haven't been. Since that night we walked along Fifth…I haven't thought about the past. I've let go of it," she said.

"Not good enough. I know you by now, Willow, and you haven't let go of anything. You've been analyzing the past and trying to figure out exactly what is best for you. And you know what? I get it. I've been doing the same."

"You have?"

"Yes. The only difference is I've been trying to convince myself to take a chance on love and take a chance on you. Only now I'm so glad I didn't."

"You are?" she asked, wishing she could come up with something else to say but she'd had no idea that this was what she'd feel like when her heart broke.

"Yes I am. I knew that I wasn't meant to share my life with another person. My experiences have all confirmed for me that life is better when you only have yourself to depend on. So thanks for reminding me once again that I'm meant to be alone."

"Jack, I didn't. I never meant—"

"I think we're done here. Would you like me to call you a cab?" he asked.

She shook her head. She could find her own way home. She looked at his face, stared at him for a good long time so she'd never forget this moment or what her own burning need for vengeance had reaped for her. Then she turned and walked to the door.

"I never meant to hurt you. I just wanted to ease the ache I had inside me for so long," she said, and then she opened the door and walked out without looking back.

Willow left Jack's apartment in a total daze. She hailed a cab but couldn't remember her address at first before finally getting it out. She'd known deep in her heart that taking a bet to get involved with someone was a sure fire way to doom but…

But what?

She got to her house, walked in the door, locked it behind her and leaned back against it as she sank to the floor. She pulled her knees up, rested her forehead on them and started crying. She'd been thinking for so long that she'd known what heartbreak was. That her sixteen-year-old self had learned all that she needed to know on the subject but Jack Crown had just shown her how wrong she had been.

At sixteen, she'd thought she understood what a broken heart had felt like, but today she realized she hadn't. She hadn't really known Jack the way she did now. She had started to put her high school puppy love for Jack in perspective when her mom died the following year, but for some reason she'd never put the two together.

And she'd never known that losing Jack would make her ache like this inside. She had known when she'd started down the path of vengeance that it wasn't going to end well for Jack, but she'd never counted the cost to herself. Now she knew better. She should have realized that Jack was the one man in the world who could sneak past her guard. There were a million tiny details she could have changed that would have given her what she now knew she wanted—Jack.

But she had been afraid to take a chance on him—and on herself. She was beginning to believe that Jack hadn't been the one to keep her from letting deep relationships form, she had.

She'd always been afraid to let anyone close in case they hurt her. The one time she took a chance, she'd done it in the one way that guaranteed she'd be hurt again. Was she some sort of emotional masochist? Did she just like being miserable?

She shook her head. Her iPhone started vibrating in her pocket and she fumbled in her coat to get it out. Maybe it was Jack. *Oh, please let it be Jack.* He could have changed his mind and decided—

It was Nichole.

She wiped the tears from her eyes, wishing she could wipe away her disappointment as easily. But she couldn't.

"It's Willow."

"Hey, are you alone?"

"Why yes, I am," she said.

"Good. I just found out that Conner mentioned our bet to Jack. I don't know if you'd told him or not but I didn't want you to be blindsided," Nic said.

She shook her head and rested it against the door. "Too late."

"Oh, no. I already told him that he was an idiot and that he should never have said anything."

"Conner isn't to blame, Nic. I am. I should never have wagered on love. When does that ever end well?"

"Then it's my fault as I'm the one who suggested it," Nichole said. She sounded upset.

"I wouldn't have gone out with him if you hadn't. I was on the verge of backing out and you knew it."

"But even if I hadn't done it maybe you eventually would have given him a chance anyway. I don't think he was going to stop asking."

"I never would have," Willow said. "I have spent my entire life hiding from any chance of a deep bond with a man, and Jack has always scared me."

"Dammit. What can we do?"

"Nothing," Willow said. "I messed this up and Jack isn't in any mood to forgive me."

"You're just giving up?" Nichole asked.

"I don't know. I don't know what else to do."

"Hold the line. We need Gail."

"We don't need—"

"Willow, you need your friends. And Gail and I have both been in your shoes. We know how it feels to lose the man you love."

"I didn't say I love him," Willow said, still clinging to the misconception that if she didn't admit it this wouldn't hurt as bad.

"That's BS and you know it. One second," Nichole said.

If even her friends knew she loved Jack why hadn't he been able to see it and just take the decision out of her hands? She wanted him to force her to admit her feelings...but why?

"Willow, honey, are you okay?" Gail asked as she came on the line.

"No," Willow admitted. "I ache with such sadness. I had no idea this was what heartbreak feels like. How could I have mistaken what I felt at sixteen for this?"

"Because you were sixteen," Gail said. "What can we do?"

"Nothing. Jack doesn't want to talk to me again. He was beyond pissed off at me. I don't think there is a single thing—"

"That's defeatist," Nichole said. "And not like you. When you got turned down by the network for *Pregnant & Proud* you didn't take no for an answer, did you?"

"No," she said. "I didn't. I went out and shot it and then sent it to them. But this is different. This isn't some committee who doesn't think that TV viewers want to see pregnant women preparing for birth. This is a man who doesn't want to see me again because I hurt him."

"Yes, you hurt him." Gail said. "Take what you are feeling and apply it to him."

"But Jack said he likes to be alone," Willow said.

"He likes it because he is safer that way. He is hurting just as much as you are right now and you owe it to him to make it up to him," Nichole said.

"What Nic is trying to say in that convoluted way of hers is that you need to go after him and show him that you love him."

"I haven't said it," Willow admitted. "I didn't want to be the first one. Listen, I'm not even sure he loves me."

"Then you are an idiot," Nichole said. "Sorry to be mean but that's the truth. The man has been showing you he cares since he first showed up on the set of *Sexy & Single* in May."

Willow thought about it for a good long minute and then sighed. They were right. If she just let him walk out of her life again she'd be dooming both of them to never finding true happiness. She just had to figure out how to make him see that she was sorry for what she'd done and that she loved him more than anything.

"You're right," she said. "I need to come up with a plan."

* * *

One of the benefits of being a celebrity and having a vast network of contacts was that when he'd decided to leave the East Coast, Jack didn't have to wait for a scheduled airline flight. He called a friend who knew someone with a G6 and the next thing he knew he was on the luxury jet heading for California.

He sat in the large leather seat nursing a Jack and Coke and wishing he could leave behind the aching in his heart as easily as he was leaving New York.

The sad part was he'd known that Willow was going to do something to hurt him. He'd known that she was just a temporary partner. Why had he let himself fall for her?

He was smarter than that and always had been. He'd carefully dated women who weren't looking for more than some good times with him because his Karma was to be alone.

And yet he'd been fixated on her like she could be more than that. Willow Stead…the woman who used her iron fist to keep everyone under her control. Except that she hadn't done that with him.

He knew that the bet she'd made wasn't her best moment and to be honest he could almost see why Nichole had done it. He'd known that night when Willow had shown up that he'd gotten lucky she hadn't backed out. But he'd thought that it had been Willow's own curiosity about what could develop between them that had brought her to his door.

In no way had he ever imagined that she'd come as the result of a wager. To be fair, she was the only woman in his world of acquaintances who would do such a thing.

He rubbed the back of his neck, finished off his drink

and reached for the bottle to pour himself another one. Then stopped. He was about to land in L.A. with a hangover.

But then he thought why the hell not? He already felt like crap inside and maybe if he drank enough Jack and Coke he'd forget the way she'd looked when she'd stood in the doorway of his apartment.

Or forget the way her hand had felt on his thigh. He threw his glass across the plane. Dammit. That was what pissed him off the most. He'd thought they had a real chance at happiness. She'd made him believe that they could be a couple—a team—and together they would navigate through life.

He felt like a sucker.

But he knew that was just anger talking. Embarrassed by his actions with the glass he went to pick it up as the flight attendant came out. "Did you drop this?"

"No, I threw it. Sorry, I'm in a bad mood."

"No problem. Can I get you another a drink?"

He shook his head. "But thanks. I don't think alcohol is the answer."

"It never is," she said. "But it helps us forget for a while."

"It does."

"If you need anything…just ring or throw another glass," she said.

He gave her a half smile and watched as she went back up front with the pilot. He had to get past feeling sorry for himself. This was his new reality and he was going to have to deal with it.

He called his agent, who took the call despite the fact that it was the middle of a holiday weekend and Jack knew the guy was with his family.

"Maury, I need you to get me more work for next

year. I want to be so busy that I never have time to go home and sleep," Jack said.

"Okay, what's brought this on?" Maury asked.

"Nothing. You know I like to work."

"I do," Maury said. "But last week you said maybe you would slow down a little and develop your own projects."

Jack had said that. He'd had some stupid idea that maybe he and Willow could do a show together. Not the matchmaking one but something new that reflected them both. It had been one of the sappier things he'd thought of.

"That was last week," Jack said.

"Okay, I'll see what I can do. I'll put out some calls today and over the weekend but I doubt we'll get any nibbles until Monday. I do know they are looking for someone to host the New Year's Eve live show on the West Coast. I hadn't brought it to you before because..."

"Because you thought I had a life, but I don't. I just have a career. I'll do the New Year's Eve thing. That'll be perfect," Jack said. Good to know he wouldn't be alone on that holiday thinking about Willow and maybe feeling sorry for himself.

"I can't help but think you're reacting to something," Maury said. "You know I'm here if you need me."

"I just need you to get me work so we both can make a lot of money," Jack said.

"Whatever, man. There is more to life than work," Maury said. "But you're the boss so I'll do what I can."

Maury hung up the phone and Jack was tempted to throw his phone across the plane the way he had the glass. There was more to life than just work but not for him.

Finally he had the proof he'd thought had been out

there the entire time. The evidence that he was meant to be alone. Willow had gotten him back for his idiotic actions when he'd been eighteen and he knew that he'd never again feel that little bit of hope in the back of his mind that he might be worthy of a relationship.

He should go after her, but his life had taught him that when something ended he had no choice but to move on. And this time would be the hardest to not go back.

His mom had always said that Jack was the luckiest boy she'd known. And he had been lucky in many things but never lucky in love.

He just wished he'd remembered that before he'd let himself fall for a woman with dark brown eyes, a soft cascade of straight black hair, and a heart that was made of stone.

Fourteen

Willow hadn't realized it would be so hard to figure out how to make up with Jack. She'd see him after Christmas when *Sexy & Single* taped their wrap-up show. And then in February when they started taping their second season. But she couldn't wait that long to see him again.

She'd never had to do anything like this before but once Gail had suggested she use the contacts and the skills she already had, it had made sense. She'd taken her time purchasing some little gifts for him, hoping that the gesture would be enough to get him to take her calls but he'd sent them back unopened.

It had hurt but instead of giving up it had made her more determined to win him over. She'd finally had to reach out to her contacts in the industry, which she'd done with Gail's help. Willow, who'd always spent so much of her life by herself trying to keep from letting anyone know that she cared, now had to bare her soul to people to get them on board.

Gail had arranged for Willow to meet with Rhia Montaine, and that proved to be the key to the entire thing. Jack just wouldn't see Willow or accept any calls from her friends. Even Russell and Conner were being ignored.

"I've just had a call from Jack's agent," Kat said, joining Willow in the temporary offices they'd set up in a hotel room in Santa Barbara. "He's not happy that you went behind his back to the head of his agency to get him to give you Jack's location. And the only way he'll forgive you is if you use another one of his clients the next season of *Sexy & Single*."

"Just hold on to the information. I haven't had a chance to talk to Matchmakers, Inc. about the prospective clients we'll be using next season."

"I know," Kat said, putting her hand on Willow's shoulder and squeezing it.

Kat left the room and Willow went over the plan in her head one more time. So much of it hinged on Jack. And she was in the one position she'd never wanted to be in. She was vulnerable to him. She needed him, and if this didn't work, she didn't care about her career or anything else because her life wouldn't be as fun or exciting without him in it.

She should have realized it sooner but she'd been blind to the fact that without Jack she didn't want to face the future.

Today she was going to take the biggest risk she'd ever taken. Today she was going to throw away pride and hope that Jack would see that she'd never hurt him the way she had in the past again.

Jack was taping a recap session with PJ Montaine on

the beach in Malibu. But Willow was being escorted there thanks to her calling in favors and making promises to everyone in the industry through Rhia.

"I'm not pleased that I was steamrolled into helping you," Rhia said, entering the room. "Jack deserves—"

"To be happy," Willow said. "I hurt him but I know he still cares about me and I aim to fix that. To make up for what I did. I know that using my contacts makes it seem like I'm manipulative but it was the only option left open to me. I've tried calling and sending gifts. He won't see me, Rhia."

"Okay," she said. "But just so you know I'm coming clean with him right away."

"Fair enough. If this doesn't work I don't think anything will."

Willow hadn't let herself think of failure at any point because she needed to believe that she could still win Jack back. That they were going to have their very own happy ending. If they didn't she was going to die inside.

"What do you need me to do?" Rhia asked.

"Well, I need your help getting that in the van and then we will just follow you to your house," Willow said.

"What is it?"

"A costume, something I think will make Jack smile and realize exactly how sorry I am."

Rhia shook her head. "I hope so. Like you said, Jack does deserve to be happy."

Willow got to her feet and started gathering all the things they needed. She had a small crew with her and they slowly got all the stuff in the van.

"Ride with me," Rhia said.

Willow got into Rhia's Toyota Prius and as they started the drive to her house Rhia took off her sunglasses. "This idea of yours—it will help Jack even if he doesn't forgive you. I was shocked when I realized that he didn't understand how many people he'd helped over the years. You know he's the one who got me and PJ together?"

"I didn't know that."

"Well, he did. Talked me into giving him another chance after PJ cheated on me. It was hard but Jack understood that PJ had been pushing to see how far he could go before he drove me away. I think that Jack might be doing the same thing with you. I know I said I was doing this because you blackmailed me, but I want Jack to have the same kind of happiness we do."

"I want that, too," Willow said. "When I started calling people they were all more than happy to do something for Jack. He feels like a loner but he's touched so many people's lives. Thanks for agreeing to let us do this at your house."

"No problem. While you're on the beach trying to make things right I'll be ensuring that everyone is ready to surprise him. I do think you're pretty clever about Jack. How'd you get to know him so well?" Rhia asked.

Willow just shrugged. It was because she loved him but she'd never said the words to Jack and she didn't want to say them to anyone else first. She needed that to be something just between them.

"I just know him now," Willow said.

Twenty minutes later as she was being led down to the beach in her costume she wondered if she knew herself as well as she thought she knew Jack because this idea terrified her. She'd never put herself out there before and this was going to be one big scary mess if Jack didn't love her the way she hoped he did.

There was a tent set up with chairs for the crew of *Extreme Careers.* The sun shone brightly. It was a good day to be in Southern California even if it was December. PJ had just gotten into position in a director's chair with the rolling surf behind them. Jack had suggested doing this on a soundstage but PJ wanted to be outside and Jack hadn't argued.

The cameramen were in position and the sound guys did one last check of the microphones before the director came over. "Dude, before we get started. There is someone here to see you. Since PJ is set up, I think you should meet them over there."

"I don't think we have time for this," Jack said, glancing in the direction that Ben had pointed. Then he did a double take.

It looked like a large green frog with a crown and a pink dress was waiting for him. Jack shook his head, unable to believe what he was seeing. But he couldn't resist going over there. He knew he shouldn't have sent back Willow's gifts but he'd been too mad when they'd first arrived and he had already decided the next time she called he'd talk to her.

But this messagegram of hers had beaten him to the punch. He had to admit he was intrigued by what she'd say through her messenger.

"Okay, this shouldn't take long," Jack said.

"Take your time, man," Ben said.

Jack walked over to the frog and then stopped.

"I'm Jack Crown."

"Yes, you are."

His brow furrowed. "Willow?"

"Yes. I'm trapped in here because I was afraid to believe in love. All the time you thought that I needed to kiss you to find Prince Charming when it was really the fact that I was the frog. I was the one who had the curse on her."

"You were?"

"Yes. That's why I acted so ridiculous," she said. She reached out and took his hand.

He stared into the fake black eyes. This was surreal.

"Jack, I'm sorry that I didn't trust you enough to just go out with you," she said. "I'm sorry I never found the courage to tell you this before, but it took losing you for me to realize that I can't live without you."

"It did?" he asked then cursed under his breath. "I can't do this staring into the eyes of a foam head. I need to see your face."

"You have to kiss me to turn me back into Willow."

"Take off the head and I will," Jack said.

She took off the head and set it on the ground. He stared down at her. He had missed her more than he'd wanted to admit. He'd been able to keep up the facade of anger during the day but each night in his dreams she'd visited him and he'd held her close.

"I miss you," she said. "All the time I was worried about you leaving me. About you heading back here after our show was done taping, and I never realized that if I didn't give you a reason to stay, well, then you wouldn't."

"What is your reasoning?" he asked, aching to reach out and hug her, to pull her to him and never let her go. But he couldn't do that. Not yet.

"I love you," she said. "I realized it that day in the Hamptons but I was so afraid to let you see it. So afraid that if I admitted it out loud then I'd be vulnerable. But it doesn't matter. I can't keep quiet anymore. I know you don't feel the same as I do."

"You're right," he said. "I feel more than you do. I love you so much I don't know how to go on without you."

"Really? Then why have you been pushing me away?"

"I had to know that I meant the same to you," he said.

"Fair enough. I love you more than I thought I could love another person," she admitted.

He couldn't wait another second, so he leaned over to kiss her. She wrapped her green costumed arms around him and held on tight. It had to be the best kiss he'd ever experienced but also the strangest.

"I'm sorry I was so stupid."

Jack shook his head. "I'm glad you were. We never would have found each other. I was getting tired of being turned down. I would have stopped asking."

"I was getting tired of saying no. I wanted an excuse to have to see you. From the moment you walked back into my life I've been attracted to you. I was just too embarrassed to admit it after the things I'd said about you."

"For my part I'm sorry I made you feel the way I did."

"You already apologized for the past. I realize now that I have to let go of that for us to have a future together. And I really want that."

"Me, too," Jack said. There was nothing he wanted more. "Is there a way to get you out of this thing?"

"Yes, but you can't do that yet. I have another surprise for you up at PJ and Rhia's."

"You do?"

"Yes, I hope you don't mind but I had to resort to blackmail to get your friends to talk to me. But once I did they all wanted to do something nice for you," Willow said.

"Really? Why?" Jack asked, not sure what friends she was talking about.

"You keep thinking you are a loner on your journey but you have touched the lives of so many people. They all wanted a chance to say thank you. And to show you that you are not alone."

"Why did you do that?" he asked, touched that she'd gone to such an extent for him.

"Even if you couldn't forgive me and love me, I wanted to show you that you are not alone."

He hugged her close, unable to speak because he was choked up. He hadn't allowed himself to dream that they could find this kind of happiness together and he knew he was never going to let her go.

Epilogue

It was January 2 and Jack and Willow were in New York to film a wrap-up session ending the first season of *Sexy & Single.* It was hard to believe as he stood in the green room munching on the exotic fruit that Kat had specifically brought over to him that six couples were now together thanks to this show.

Conner waved at Jack as he entered the room. He wasn't going to be part of the taping but had come down today with Nichole because after they were done Gail, Russell, Nichole, Conner, Willow and himself were heading to the Bahamas for a week's vacation.

"Jack, we haven't had a chance to talk alone, but I wanted to apologize for my part in the mess with you and Willow," Conner said, coming over to shake his hand.

"You have nothing to apologize for. I never held you responsible in any way," Jack said.

"I'm glad. I felt like an idiot afterward," Conner said.

"Don't. I needed to know what Willow had done," Jack said.

"I'm glad there are no hard feelings," Conner said. "I heard through the grapevine you made an offer on a house in the Hamptons."

"I did. But what grapevine? Contracts haven't even been signed yet," Jack asked.

"Mother. She has her finger on all the gossip out there," Conner said with a laugh. Nichole came into the room, positively glowing in her designer maternity dress. Her thick red hair hung in soft waves to her shoulders and she smiled over at Conner with such love and tenderness that Jack had to look away.

"Later," Conner said, walking over to his wife and pulling her into his arms to kiss her.

"Hello, everyone," Fiona McCaw-Cannon said as she entered the room at a very slow pace, leading Bella Ann by the hand. Alex was at the baby's side, holding her other little hand in his.

"Hello," Jack said. "I see Bella Ann has grown."

"Yes, and she can talk now," Alex said, beaming down at his stepdaughter like she was the most clever person he knew. Alex scooped the baby up and turned to Jack. "Say hello to Jack."

"Hello," the little girl said. She waved over at him but in that backward way that kids did so it looked like she was waving at herself.

Fiona laughed. "He's such a proud papa."

Alex snaked his arm around his wife and kissed her on the cheek. "When a man is as lucky as I am he's bound to brag about it."

"Fair enough," Fiona said.

"I guess it's safe to say you are both happy with Matchmakers, Inc.," Conner said.

"Definitely. I have recommended your company to a number of my friends," Fiona said.

Next to enter the room were Rikki and Paul, the third couple to be on the show. Rikki was a party planner who was even more of a control freak than Willow, Jack thought. But quiet, mild-mannered corporate lawyer Paul had found a way to tame her. Deidre and Peter entered and both of them gave him a little wave before the soundman drew them away to be fitted with microphones. They were headed to Peter's home in Raleigh-Durham after the taping for a little one-on-one time before the racing season started. Because Deidre worked from home writing her advice columns, she planned to travel to all of the races with Peter this year.

"Before we go in for the taping," Peter said, coming over to him, "I wanted to let you know that I asked Deidre to marry me on New Year's Eve and she said yes. We'll be getting married next November after my racing season ends."

"Congratulations," Jack said, shaking the other man's hand. "Willow and I are engaged as well. I asked her at Christmas."

"Given that he had to work New Year's," Willow said, coming up behind him, "that was his only option."

Jack gave her a hug and she hugged him back. He had never thought he could be as happy with another person as he was with Willow. Every day together they'd grown more comfortable with their love and both of them were relaxing their guard around each other.

"Gail and Russell are in the building and will be up here in a minute. I need everyone to start making their way to the set so we can get in position," Willow said.

"Conner, there's still time for you to change your mind and join us," Willow said

"No way. I'm still more comfortable being a recluse."

"Yes, you are," Nichole said, giving him a kiss.

The rest of the couples left the room to go to the set as Russell and Gail entered. "Sorry we're late. We just came from the adoption agency...."

"Yes?" Nichole asked.

"They have a child for us. Two children, actually. A three-year-old girl and her eighteen-month-old brother," Russell said. "I hope you don't mind but that took precedence over getting here on time."

"Congratulations," Willow said as she and Nichole hugged Gail.

Conner and Russell looked at Jack and he just shook his head. "I'm not hugging you, dude, but I'm happy for you."

"Thanks," Russell said. "I wasn't about to let you hug me, mate."

Conner just shook his head.

"Let's go, you guys. Everyone wants to get this shoot done so they can get back to their lives," Kat said, coming in.

"We're coming," Willow said.

But when Jack started to follow them, she caught his hand and pulled him to a stop. "Thank you."

"For?"

"Being so stubborn and not letting me keep saying no to you," she said.

He pulled her into his arms and kissed her long and hard. "You are very welcome. It seems once again I was right."

"Right?"

"You can't live without me," he said.

"And you can't live without me," she said. "I guess that makes us even."

It didn't feel even to him. Willow had given him something that he'd never thought was missing in his life and he was so happy to have her as his own.

* * * * *

COMING NEXT MONTH from Harlequin Desire®
AVAILABLE NOVEMBER 27, 2012

#2197 ONE WINTER'S NIGHT
The Westmorelands
Brenda Jackson

Riley Westmoreland never mixes business with pleasure—until he meets his company's gorgeous new party planner and realizes one night will never be enough.

#2198 A GOLDEN BETRAYAL
The Highest Bidder
Barbara Dunlop

The head of a New York auction house is swept off her feet by the crown prince of a desert kingdom who has accused her of trafficking in stolen goods!

#2199 STAKING HIS CLAIM
Billionaires and Babies
Tessa Radley

She never planned a baby...he doesn't plan to let his baby go. The solution should be simple. But no one told Ella that love is the riskiest business of all....

#2200 BECOMING DANTE
The Dante Legacy
Day Leclaire

Gabe Moretti discovers he's not just a Moretti—he's a secret Dante. Now the burning passion—the Inferno—for Kat Malloy won't be ignored....

#2201 THE SHEIKH'S DESTINY
Desert Knights
Olivia Gates

Marrying Laylah is Rashid's means to the throne. But when she discovers his plot and casts him from her heart, will claiming the throne mean anything if he loses her?

#2202 THE DEEPER THE PASSION...
The Drummond Vow
Jennifer Lewis

When Vicki St. Cyr is forced to ask the man who broke her heart for help in claiming a reward, old passions and long-buried emotions flare.

You can find more information on upcoming Harlequin® titles, free excerpts and more at www.Harlequin.com.

HDCNM1112

REQUEST YOUR FREE BOOKS!

2 FREE NOVELS PLUS 2 FREE GIFTS!

ALWAYS POWERFUL, PASSIONATE AND PROVOCATIVE

YES! Please send me 2 FREE Harlequin Desire® novels and my 2 FREE gifts (gifts are worth about $10). After receiving them, if I don't wish to receive any more books, I can return the shipping statement marked "cancel." If I don't cancel, I will receive 6 brand-new novels every month and be billed just $4.30 per book in the U.S. or $4.99 per book in Canada. That's a saving of at least 14% off the cover price! It's quite a bargain! Shipping and handling is just 50¢ per book in the U.S. and 75¢ per book in Canada.* I understand that accepting the 2 free books and gifts places me under no obligation to buy anything. I can always return a shipment and cancel at any time. Even if I never buy another book, the two free books and gifts are mine to keep forever.

225/326 HDN FEF3

Name (PLEASE PRINT)

Address Apt. #

City State/Prov. Zip/Postal Code

Signature (if under 18, a parent or guardian must sign)

Mail to the **Reader Service:**

IN U.S.A.: P.O. Box 1867, Buffalo, NY 14240-1867
IN CANADA: P.O. Box 609, Fort Erie, Ontario L2A 5X3

Not valid for current subscribers to Harlequin Desire books.

Want to try two free books from another line?
Call 1-800-873-8635 or visit www.ReaderService.com.

* Terms and prices subject to change without notice. Prices do not include applicable taxes. Sales tax applicable in N.Y. Canadian residents will be charged applicable taxes. Offer not valid in Quebec. This offer is limited to one order per household. All orders subject to credit approval. Credit or debit balances in a customer's account(s) may be offset by any other outstanding balance owed by or to the customer. Please allow 4 to 6 weeks for delivery. Offer available while quantities last.

Your Privacy—The Reader Service is committed to protecting your privacy. Our Privacy Policy is available online at www.ReaderService.com or upon request from the Reader Service.

We make a portion of our mailing list available to reputable third parties that offer products we believe may interest you. If you prefer that we not exchange your name with third parties, or if you wish to clarify or modify your communication preferences, please visit us at www.ReaderService.com/consumerschoice or write to us at Reader Service Preference Service, P.O. Box 9062, Buffalo, NY 14269. Include your complete name and address.

HDES11B

Harlequin® Desire is proud to present

ONE WINTER'S NIGHT

by New York Times *bestselling author*

Brenda Jackson

Alpha Blake tightened her coat around her. Not only would she be late for her appointment with Riley Westmoreland, but because of her flat tire they would have to change the location of the meeting and Mr. Westmoreland would be the one driving her there. This was totally embarrassing, when she had been trying to make a good impression.

She turned up the heat in her car. Even with a steady stream of hot air coming in through the car vents, she still felt cold, too cold, and wondered if she would ever get used to the Denver weather. Of course, it was too late to think about that now. It was her first winter here, and she didn't have any choice but to grin and bear it. When she'd moved, she'd felt that getting as far away from Daytona Beach as she could was essential to her peace of mind. But who in her right mind would prefer blistering-cold Denver to sunny Daytona Beach? Only a person wanting to start a new life and put a painful past behind her.

Her attention was snagged by an SUV that pulled off the road and parked in front of her. The door swung open and long denim-clad, boot-wearing legs appeared before a man stepped out of the truck. She met his gaze through the windshield and forgot to breathe. Walking toward her car was a man who was so dangerously masculine, so heart-stoppingly virile, that her brain went momentarily numb.

He was tall, and the Stetson on his head made him appear taller. But his height was secondary to the sharp

HDEXP1212

handsomeness of his features.

Her gaze slid all over him as he moved his long limbs toward her vehicle in a walk that was so agile and self-assured, she envied the confidence he exuded with every step. Her breasts suddenly peaked, and she could actually feel blood rushing through her veins.

She didn't have to guess who this man was.

He was Riley Westmoreland.

Find out if Riley and Alpha mix business with pleasure in

ONE WINTER'S NIGHT

by Brenda Jackson

Available December 2012

Only from Harlequin® Desire

Copyright © 2012 by Brenda Streater Jackson

HDEXP1212

SPECIAL EDITION

Life, Love and Family

NEW YORK TIMES **BESTSELLING AUTHOR**

DIANA PALMER

brings you a brand-new Western romance featuring characters that readers have come to love—the Brannt family from Harlequin HQN's bestselling book *WYOMING TOUGH*.

Cort Brannt, Texas rancher through and through, is about to unexpectedly get lassoed by love!

THE RANCHER

Available November 13 wherever books are sold!

Also available as a 2-in-1

THE RANCHER & HEART OF STONE

www.Harlequin.com

HSE65709DP